THE

EPICUREAN

A TALE

BY

THOMAS MOORE

© 2023 Culturea Editions
Illustration de couverture : © domaine public
Edition : Culturea, le patrimoine des lettres (Hérault, 34)
Contact : infos@culturea.fr
Retrouvez notre catalogue sur http://culturea.fr
Imprimé en Allemagne par Books on Demand, In de Tarpen 42, Norderstedt
Design typographique : Derek Murphy
Layout : Reedsy (https://reedsy.com/)
ISBN : 9791041940332
Dépôt légal : janvier 2023
Tous droits réservés pour tous pays

A

LETTER TO THE TRANSLATOR,

FROM

——, Esq.

Cairo, June 19. 1800.

My dear Sir,

In a visit I lately paid to the monastery of St. Macarius,—which is situated, as you know, in the Valley of the Lakes of Natron,—I was lucky enough to obtain possession of a curious Greek manuscript, which, in the hope that you may be induced to translate it, I herewith send you. Observing one of the monks very busily occupied in tearing up, into a variety of fantastic shapes, some papers which had the appearance of being the [vi] leaves of old books, I enquired of him the meaning of his task, and received the following explanation:——

The Arabs, it seems, who are as fond of pigeons as the ancient Egyptians, have a superstitious notion that, if they place in their pigeon-houses small scraps of paper, written over with learned characters, the birds are always sure to thrive the better for the charm; and the monks, who are never slow in profiting by superstition, have, at all times, a supply of such amulets for purchasers.

In general, the holy fathers have been in the habit of scribbling these mystic fragments, themselves; but a discovery, which they have lately made, saves them this trouble. Having dug up (as

my informant stated) a chest of old manuscripts, which, being
chiefly on the subject of alchemy, must have been buried in the
time of Dioclesian, "we thought we could not," added the monk,
"employ such rubbish more properly, than in tearing it up, as you
see, for the pigeon-houses of the Arabs."

On my expressing a wish to rescue some part of these treasures
from the fate to which his indolent fraternity had consigned them,
he produced the manuscript which I have now the pleasure of
sending you,—the only one, he said, remaining entire,—and I
very readily paid him the price he demanded for it.

You will find the story, I think, not altogether uninteresting;
and the coincidence, in many respects, of the curious details in
Chap. VI. with the description of the same ceremonies in the
Romance of *Sethos*[1], will, I have no doubt, strike you. Hoping
that you may be tempted to give a translation of this Tale to the
world,

I am, my dear Sir,
Very truly yours,

_____

_____

[1] The description, here alluded to, may also be found, copied *verbatim* from
Sethos, in the "Voyages d'Anténor."—"In that philosophical romance, called
'La Vie de Séthos,'" says Warburton, "we find a much juster account of old
Egyptian wisdom, than in all the pretended 'Histoire du Ciel.'" *Div. Leg.* book
4. sect. 14.

THE EPICUREAN.

CHAPTER I.

It was in the fourth year of the reign of the late Emperor Valerian, that the followers of Epicurus, who were at that time numerous in Athens, proceeded to the election of a person to fill the vacant chair of their sect;—and, by the unanimous voice of the School, I was the individual chosen for their Chief. I was just then entering on my twenty-fourth year, and no instance had ever before occurred, of a person so young being selected for that office. Youth, however, and the personal advantages that adorn it, were not, it may be supposed, among the least valid recommendations, to a sect that included within its circle all the beauty as well as wit of Athens, and which, though dignifying its pursuits with the [2] name of philosophy, was little else than a pretext for the more refined cultivation of pleasure.

The character of the sect had, indeed, much changed, since the time of its wise and virtuous founder, who, while he asserted that Pleasure is the only Good, inculcated also that Good is the only source of Pleasure. The purer part of this doctrine had long evaporated, and the temperate Epicurus would have as little recognised his own sect in the assemblage of refined voluptuaries who now usurped its name, as he would have known his own quiet Garden in the luxurious groves and bowers among which the meetings of the School were now held.

Many causes, besides the attractiveness of its doctrines, con-
curred, at this period, to render our school the most popular of
any that still survived the glory of Greece. It may generally be
observed, that the prevalence, in one half of a community, of very
rigid notions on the subject of religion, produces the opposite
extreme of laxity and infidelity in the other; and this kind of
re-action it was that now mainly contributed to render the doctrines of the Garden the most fashionable philosophy of the day.
The rapid progress of the Christian faith had alarmed all those,
who, either from piety or worldliness, were interested in the
continuance of the old established creed—all who believed in the
Deities of Olympus, and all who lived by them. The consequence
was, a considerable increase of zeal and activity, throughout
the constituted authorities and priesthood of the whole Heathen
world. What was wanting in sincerity of belief was made up
in rigour;—the weakest parts of the Mythology were those, of
course, most angrily defended, and any reflections, tending to
bring Saturn, or his wife Ops, into contempt, were punished with
the utmost severity of the law.

In this state of affairs, between the alarmed bigotry of the
declining Faith, and the simple, sublime austerity of her rival, it
was not wonderful that those lovers of ease and pleasure, who
had no interest, reversionary or otherwise, in the old religion,
and were too indolent to enquire into the sanctions of the new,
should take refuge from the severities of both under the shelter
of a luxurious philosophy, which, leaving to others the task of
disputing about the future, centered all its wisdom in the full
enjoyment of the present.

The sectaries of the Garden had, ever since the death of their
founder, been accustomed to dedicate to his memory the twen-
tieth day of every month. To these monthly rites had, for some
time, been added a grand annual Festival, in commemoration of
his birth. The feasts, given on this occasion by my predecessors
in the Chair, had been invariably distinguished for their taste

[3]

[4]

and splendour; and it was my ambition, not merely to imitate this example, but even to render the anniversary, now celebrated under my auspices, so brilliant, as to efface the recollection of all that went before it. [5]

Seldom, indeed, had Athens witnessed such a scene. The grounds that formed the original site of the Garden had, from time to time, received considerable additions; and the whole extent was laid out with that perfect taste, which knows how to wed Nature to Art, without sacrificing her simplicity to the alliance. Walks, leading through wildernesses of shade and fragrance—glades, opening, as if to afford a play-ground for the sunshine—temples, rising on the very spots where imagination herself would have called them up, and fountains and lakes, in alternate motion and repose, either wantonly courting the ver-dure, or calmly sleeping in its embrace,—such was the variety of feature that diversified these fair gardens; and, animated as they were on this occasion, by all the living wit and loveliness of Athens, it afforded a scene such as my own youthful fancy, rich as it was then in images of luxury and beauty, could hardly have anticipated. [6]

The ceremonies of the day began with the very dawn, when, according to the form of simpler and better times, those among the disciples who had apartments within the Garden, bore the image of our Founder in procession from chamber to chamber, chanting verses in praise of—what had long ceased to be objects of our imitation—his frugality and temperance.

Round a beautiful lake, in the centre of the garden, stood four white Doric temples, in one of which was collected a library containing all the flowers of Grecian literature; while, in the remaining three, Conversation, the Song, and the Dance, held, uninterrupted by each other, their respective rites. In the Library stood busts of all the most illustrious Epicureans, both of Rome and Greece—Horace, Atticus, Pliny the elder, the poet Lucretius, Lucian, and the biographer of the Philosophers, lately lost to us,

Diogenes Laertius. There were also the portraits, in marble, of all the eminent female votaries of the school—Leontium and her fair daughter Danae, Themista, Philænis, and others.

It was here that, in my capacity of Heresiarch, on the morning of the Festival, I received the felicitations of the day from some of the fairest lips of Athens; and, in pronouncing the customary oration to the memory of our Master (in which it was usual to dwell on the doctrines he inculcated) endeavoured to attain that art, so useful before such an audience, of diffusing over the gravest subjects a charm, which secures them listeners even among the simplest and most volatile.

Though study, as may easily be supposed, engrossed but little of the mornings of the Garden, yet the lighter part of learning,—that portion of its attic honey, for which the bee is not obliged to go very deep into the flower—was zealously cultivated. Even here, however, the student had to encounter distractions, which are, of all others, least favourable to composure of thought; and, with more than one of my fair disciples, there used to occur such scenes as the following, which a poet of the Garden, taking his picture from the life, described:—

"As o'er the lake, in evening's glow,
    That temple threw its lengthening shade,
Upon the marble steps below,
    There sate a fair Corinthian maid,
Gracefully o'er some volume bending;
    While, by her side, the youthful Sage
Held back her ringlets, lest, descending,
    They should o'er-shadow all the page."

But it was for the evening of that day, that the richest of our luxuries were reserved. Every part of the Garden was illuminated, with the most skilful variety of lustre; while over the Lake of the Temples were scattered wreaths of flowers, through which boats, filled with beautiful children, floated, as through a liquid parterre.

Between two of these boats a perpetual combat was maintained;—their respective commanders, two blooming youths, [9] being habited to represent Eros and Anteros; the former, the Celestial Love of the Platonists, and the latter, that more earthly spirit, which usurps the name of Love among the Epicureans. Throughout the evening their conflict was carried on with various success; the timid distance at which Eros kept from his more lively antagonist being his only safeguard against those darts of fire, with showers of which the other continually assailed him, but which, luckily falling short of their mark upon the lake, only scorched the flowers upon which they fell, and were extinguished.

In another part of the gardens, on a wide verdant glade, lighted only by the moon, an imitation of the torch-race of the Panathenæa was performed, by young boys chosen for their fleetness, and arrayed with wings, like Cupids; while, not far off, a group of seven nymphs, with each a star on her forehead, represented the movements of the planetary choir, and embodied the dream [10] of Pythagoras into real motion and song.

At every turning some new enchantment broke upon the ear or eye. Sometimes, from the depth of a grove, from which a fountain at the same time issued, there came a strain of music, which, mingling with the murmur of the water, seemed like the voice of the spirit that presided over its flow;—while sometimes the strain rose breathing from among flowers; and, again, would appear to come suddenly from under ground, as if the foot had just touched some spring that set it in motion.

It seems strange that I should now dwell upon these minute descriptions; but every thing connected with that memorable night—even its long-repented follies—must for ever live sacredly in my memory. The festival concluded with a banquet, at which I, of course, presided; and, feeling myself to be the ascendant spirit of the whole scene, gave life to all around me, and saw my own happiness reflected in that of others.

CHAP. II.

The festival was over;—the sounds of the song and dance had ceased, and I was now left in those luxurious gardens, alone. Though so ardent and active a votary of pleasure, I had, by nature, a disposition full of melancholy;—an imagination that presented sad thoughts, even in the midst of mirth and happiness, and threw the shadow of the future over the gayest illusions of the present. Melancholy was, indeed, twin-born in my soul with Passion; and, not even in the fullest fervour of the latter, were they separated. From the first moment that I was conscious of thought and feeling, the same dark thread had run across the web; and images of death and annihilation mingled themselves with the most smiling scenes through which my career of enjoyment led me. My very passion for pleasure but deepened these gloomy fancies. For, shut out, as I was by my creed, from a future life, [12] and having no hope beyond the narrow horizon of this, every minute of delight assumed a mournful preciousness in my eyes, and pleasure, like the flower of the cemetery, grew but more luxuriant from the neighbourhood of death.

This very night my triumph, my happiness had seemed complete. I had been the presiding genius of that voluptuous scene. Both my ambition and my love of pleasure had drunk deep of the cup for which they thirsted. Looked up to by the learned, and loved by the beautiful and the young, I had seen, in every eye that met mine, either the acknowledgment of triumphs already won, or the promise of others, still brighter, that awaited me. Yet, even in the midst of all this, the same dark thoughts

had presented themselves;—the perishableness of myself and all
around me every instant recurred to my mind. Those hands I had
prest—those eyes, in which I had seen sparkling, a spirit of light
and life that should never die—those voices, that had talked of
eternal love—all, all, I felt, were but a mockery of the moment,
and would leave nothing eternal but the silence of their dust!

[13]

> Oh, were it not for this sad voice,
>   Stealing amid our mirth to say,
> That all, in which we most rejoice,
>   Ere night may be the earth-worm's prey;—
> *But* for this bitter—only this—
> Full as the world is brimm'd with bliss,
> And capable as feels my soul
> Of draining to its depth the whole,
> I should turn earth to heaven, and be,
> If bliss made gods, a deity!

Such was the description I gave of my own feelings, in one of
those wild, passionate songs, to which this ferment of my spirits,
between mirth and melancholy, gave birth.

Seldom had my heart more fully abandoned itself to such
vague sadness than at the present moment, when, as I paced
thoughtfully among the fading lights and flowers of the banquet,
the echo of my own step was all that sounded, where so many
gay forms had lately been revelling. The moon was still up, the
morning had not yet glimmered, and the calm glories of night
still rested on all around. Unconscious whither my pathway led,
I wandered along, till I, at length, found myself before that fair
statue of Venus, with which the chisel of Alcamenes had embellished our Garden;—that image of deified woman, the only idol
to which I had ever bent the knee. Leaning against the pedestal,
I raised my eyes to heaven, and fixing them sadly and intently
on the ever-burning stars, as if I sought to read the mournful
secret in their light, asked, wherefore was it that Man alone must

[14]

perish, while they, less wonderful, less glorious than he, lived on in light unchangeable and for ever!—"Oh, that there were some spell, some talisman," I exclaimed, "to make the spirit within us deathless as those stars, and open to its desires a career like [15] theirs, burning and boundless throughout all time!"

While I gave myself up to this train of thought, that lassitude which earthly pleasure, however sweet, leaves behind,—as if to show how earthly it is,—came drowsily over me, and I sunk at the base of the statue to sleep.

Even in sleep, however, my fancy was still busy; and a dream, so vivid as to leave behind it the impression of reality, thus passed through my mind. I thought myself transported to a wide desert plain, where nothing seemed to breathe, or move, or live. The very sky above it looked pale and extinct, giving the idea, not of darkness, but of light that had died; and, had that region been the remains of some older world, left broken up and sunless, it could not have looked more dead and desolate. The only thing that bespoke life, in this melancholy waste, was a small moving spark, that at first glimmered in the distance, but, at length, [16] slowly approached the spot where I stood. As it drew nearer, I could perceive that its feeble gleam was from a taper in the hand of a pale venerable man, who now stood, like a messenger from the grave, before me. After a few moments of awful silence, during which he looked at me with a sadness that thrilled my very soul, he said,—"Thou, who seekest eternal life, go unto the shores of the dark Nile—go unto the shores of the dark Nile, and thou wilt find the eternal life thou seekest!"

No sooner had he said these words than the death-like hue of his cheek brightened into a smile of more than human promise. The small torch that he held sent forth a radiance, by which suddenly the whole surface of the desert was illuminated, even to the far horizon's edge, along whose line were now seen gardens, palaces, and spires, all bright and golden, like the architecture of the clouds at sunset. Sweet music, too, was heard every where,

[17]

floating around, and, from all sides, such varieties of splendour poured, that, with the excess both of harmony and of light, I woke.

That infidels should be superstitious is an anomaly neither unusual nor strange. A belief in superhuman agency seems natural and necessary to the mind; and, if not suffered to flow in the obvious channels, it will find a vent in some other. Hence, many who have doubted the existence of a God, have yet implicitly placed themselves under the patronage of Fate or the stars. Much the same inconsistency I was conscious of in my own feelings. Though rejecting all belief in a Divine Providence, I had yet a faith in dreams, that all my philosophy could not conquer. Nor was experience wanting to confirm me in my delusion; for, by some of those accidental coincidences, which make the fortune of soothsayers and prophets, dreams, more than once, had been to me

Oracles, truer far than oak,
Or dove, or tripod, ever spoke.

[18]

It was not wonderful, therefore, that the vision of that night, touching, as it did, a chord so ready to vibrate, should have affected me with more than ordinary power, and sunk deeper into my memory with every effort I made to forget it. In vain did I mock at my own weakness;—such self-derision is seldom sincere. In vain did I pursue my accustomed pleasures. Their zest was, as usual, for ever new; but still came the saddening consciousness of mortality, and, with it, the recollection of this visionary promise, to which my fancy, in defiance of my reason, still clung.

Sometimes indulging in reveries, that were little else than a continuation of my dream, I even contemplated the possible existence of some secret, by which youth might be, if not perpetuated, at least prolonged, and that dreadful vicinity of death, within whose circle love pines and pleasure sickens, might be for a while averted. "Who knows," I would ask, "but that in Egypt, that land of wonders, where Mystery hath yet unfolded but half [19] her treasures,—where so many dark secrets of the antediluvian world still remain, undeciphered, upon the pillars of Seth—who knows but some charm, some amulet, may lie hid, whose discovery, as this phantom hath promised, but waits my coming—some compound of the same pure atoms, that scintillate in the eternal stars, and whose infusion into the frame of man might make him, too, fadeless and immortal!"

Thus did I fondly speculate, in those rambling moods, when the life of excitement which I led, acting upon a warm heart and vivid fancy, produced an intoxication of spirit, during which I was not wholly myself. This bewilderment, too, was not a little increased by the constant struggle between my own natural feelings, and the cold, mortal creed of my sect, in endeavouring to escape from whose deadening bondage I but broke loose into the realms of romance and fantasy.

Even, however, in my calmest and soberest moments, that strange vision perpetually haunted me. In vain were all my [20] efforts to chase it from my mind; and the deliberate conclusion to which I came at last, was, that without, at least, a visit to Egypt, I could not rest, nor, till convinced of my folly by disappointment, be reasonable. I, therefore, announced without delay to my associates of the Garden, the intention which I had formed to pay a visit to the land of Pyramids. To none of them did I dare to confess the vague, visionary impulse that actuated me. Knowledge was the object that I alleged, while Pleasure was that for which they gave me credit. The interests of the School, it was apprehended, would suffer by my absence; and there were some tenderer ties, which had still more to fear from separation. But for the former inconvenience a temporary remedy was provided; while the latter a skilful distribution of vows and sighs alleviated. Being furnished with recommendatory letters to all parts of Egypt, in the summer of the year 257, A.D. I set sail for

Alexandria.

CHAP. III.

To one, who extracted such sweets from every moment on land, a sea-voyage, however smooth and favourable, appeared the least agreeable mode of losing time that could be devised. Often did my imagination, in passing some isle of those seas, people it with fair forms and kind hearts, to whom most willingly, if I might, would I have paused to pay homage. But the wind blew direct towards the land of Mystery; and, still more, I heard a voice within me, whispering for ever "On."

As we approached the coast of Egypt, our course became less prosperous; and we had a specimen of the benevolence of the divinities of the Nile, in the shape of a storm, or rather whirlwind, which had nearly sunk our vessel, and which, the Egyptians on board said, was the work of their God, Typhon. After a day and night of danger, during which we were driven out of our course [22] to the eastward, some benigner influence prevailed above; and, at length, as the morning freshly broke, we saw the beautiful city of Alexandria rising from the sea, with its Palace of Kings, its portico of four hundred columns, and the fair Pillar of Pillars, towering up to heaven in the midst.

After passing in review this splendid vision, we shot rapidly round the Rock of Pharos, and, in a few minutes, found ourselves in the harbour of Eunostus. The sun had risen, but the light on the Great Tower of the Rock was still burning; and there was a languor in the first waking movements of that voluptuous city—whose houses and temples lay shining in silence round the harbour—that sufficiently attested the festivities of the preceding night.

[23]

We were soon landed on the quay; and, as I walked, through a line of palaces and shrines, up the street which leads from the sea to the Gate of Canopus, fresh as I was from the contemplation of my own lovely Athens, I felt a glow of admiration at the scene around me, which its novelty, even more than its magnificence, inspired. Nor were the luxuries and delights, which such a city promised, among the least of the considerations on which my fancy, at that moment, dwelt. On the contrary, every thing around seemed prophetic of future pleasure. The very forms of the architecture, to my Epicurean imagination, appeared to call up images of living grace; and even the dim seclusion of the temples and groves spoke only of tender mysteries to my mind. As the whole bright scene grew animated around me, I felt that though Egypt might not enable me to lengthen life, she could teach the next best art,—that of multiplying its enjoyments.

[24]

The population of Alexandria, at this period, consisted of the most motley miscellany of nations, religions, and sects, that had ever been brought together in one city. Beside the school of the Grecian Platonist was seen the oratory of the cabalistic Jew; while the church of the Christian stood, undisturbed, over the crypts of the Egyptian Hierophant. Here, the adorer of Fire, from the east, laughed at the superstition of the worshipper of cats, from the west. Here Christianity, too, unluckily, had learned to emulate the vagaries of Paganism; and while, on one side, her Ophite professor was seen kneeling down gravely before his serpent, on the other, a Nicosian was, as gravely, contending that there was no chance of salvation out of the pale of the Greek alphabet. Still worse, the uncharitableness of Christian schism was already distinguishing itself with equal vigour; and I heard of nothing, on my arrival, but the rancour and hate, with which the Greek and Latin churchmen persecuted each other, because, forsooth, the one fasted on the seventh day of the week, and the

[25]

others fasted upon the fourth and sixth!

To none of those religions or sects, however, except for

purposes of ridicule, did I pay much attention. I was now in the most luxurious city of the universe, and gave way, without reserve, to the seductions that surrounded me. My reputation, as a philosopher and a man of pleasure, had preceded me; and Alexandria, the second Athens of the world, welcomed me as her own. My celebrity, indeed, was as a talisman, that opened hearts and doors at my approach. The usual noviciate of acquaintance was dispensed with in my favour, and not only intimacies, but loves and friendships, ripened in my path, as rapidly as vegetation springs up where the Nile has flowed. The dark beauty of the Egyptian women had a novelty in my eyes that enhanced its other charms; and that hue of the sun on their rounded cheeks was but an earnest of the ardour he had kindled in their hearts—

Th' imbrowning of the fruit, that tells
How rich within the soul of sweetness dwells.

[26]

Some weeks rolled on in such perpetual and ever-changing pleasures, that even the melancholy voice in my heart, though it still spoke, was but seldom listened to, and soon died away in the sound of the siren songs that surrounded me. At length, however, as the novelty of these scenes wore off, the same gloomy bodings began to mingle with all my joys; and an incident that occurred, during one of my gayest revels, conduced still more to deepen their gloom.

The celebration of the annual festival of Serapis took place during my stay, and I was, more than once, induced to mingle with the gay multitudes, that crowded to his shrine at Canopus on the occasion. Day and night, while this festival lasted, the canal, which led from Alexandria to Canopus, was covered with boats full of pilgrims of both sexes, all hastening to avail themselves of this pious licence, which lent the zest of a religious sanction to pleasure, and gave a holiday to the passions of earth, in honour of heaven.

[27]

I was returning, one lovely night, to Alexandria. The north wind, that welcome visitor, freshened the air, while the banks, on either side, sent forth, from groves of orange and henna, the most delicious odours. As I had left all the crowd behind me at Canopus, there was not a boat to be seen on the canal but my own; and I was just yielding to the thoughts which solitude at such an hour inspires, when my reveries were broken by the sound of some female voices, coming, mingled with laughter and screams, from the garden of a pavilion, that stood, brilliantly illuminated, upon the bank of the canal.

On rowing nearer, I perceived that both the mirth and the alarm had been caused by the efforts of some playful girls to reach a hedge of jasmin which grew near the water, and in bending towards which they had nearly fallen into the stream. Hastening to proffer my assistance, I soon recognised the voice of one of [28] my fair Alexandrian friends, and, springing on the bank, was surrounded by the whole group, who insisted on my joining their party in the pavilion, and flinging the tendrils of jasmin, which they had just plucked, around me, led me, no unwilling captive, to the banquet-room.

I found here an assemblage of the very flower of Alexandrian society. The unexpectedness of the meeting gave it an additional zest on both sides; and seldom had I felt more enlivened myself, or contributed more successfully to circulate life among others.

Among the company were some Greek women, who, according to the fashion of their country, wore veils; but, as usual, rather to set off than conceal their beauty, some gleams of which were continually escaping from under the cloud. There was, however, one female, who particularly attracted my attention, on whose head was a chaplet of dark-coloured flowers, and who sat [29] veiled and silent during the whole of the banquet. She took no share, I observed, in what was passing around: the viands and the wine went by her untouched, nor did a word that was spoken seem addressed to her ear. This abstraction from a scene so sparkling with gaiety, though apparently unnoticed by any one but myself, struck me as mysterious and strange. I inquired of my fair neighbour the cause of it, but she looked grave and was silent.

In the mean time, the lyre and the cup went round; and a young maid from Athens, as if inspired by the presence of her countryman, took her lute, and sung to it some of the songs of Greece, with a feeling that bore me back to the banks of the Ilissus, and, even in the bosom of present pleasure, drew a sigh from my heart for that which had passed away. It was daybreak ere our delighted party rose, and unwillingly re-embarked to return to the city.

Scarcely were we afloat, when it was discovered that the lute of the young Athenian had been left behind; and, with my heart [30] still full of its sweet sounds, I most readily sprung on shore to seek it. I hastened to the banquet-room, which was now dim and solitary, except that—there, to my astonishment, still sat that silent figure, which had awakened my curiosity so strongly during the night. A vague feeling of awe came over me, as I now slowly approached it. There was no motion, no sound of breathing in that form;—not a leaf of the dark chaplet on its brow stirred. By the light of a dying lamp which stood before the figure, I raised, with a hesitating hand, the veil, and saw—what my fancy had already anticipated—that the shape underneath was lifeless, was a skeleton! Startled and shocked, I hurried back with the lute to the boat, and was almost as silent as that shape for the remainder of the voyage.

This custom among the Egyptians of placing a mummy, or skeleton, at the banquet-table, had been for some time disused, except at particular ceremonies; and, even on such occasions, it [31] had been the practice of the luxurious Alexandrians to disguise this memorial of mortality in the manner just described. But to me, who was wholly unprepared for such a spectacle, it gave a shock from which my imagination did not speedily recover. This silent and ghastly witness of mirth seemed to embody, as it were, the shadow in my own heart. The features of the grave were now stamped on the idea that haunted me, and this picture of what I *was to be* mingled itself with the sunniest aspect of what I *was*.

The memory of the dream now recurred to me more livelily than ever. The bright assuring smile of that venerable Spirit, and his words, "Go to the shores of the dark Nile, and thou wilt find the eternal life thou seekest," were for ever before my mind. But as yet, alas, I had done nothing towards realising this splendid promise. Alexandria was not Egypt;—the very soil on which it stood was not in existence, when Thebes and Memphis already counted ages of glory.

"It is beneath the Pyramids of Memphis," I exclaimed, "or in the mystic Halls of the Labyrinth, that I must seek those holy arcana of science, of which the antediluvian world has made Egypt its heir, and among which—blest thought!—the key to eternal life may lie."

Having formed my determination, I took leave of my many Alexandrian friends, and departed for Memphis.

[32]

CHAP. IV.

Egypt was the country, of all others, from that mixture of the melancholy and the voluptuous, which marked the character of her people, her religion, and her scenery, to affect deeply a temperament and fancy like mine, and keep tremblingly alive the sensibilities of both. Wherever I turned, I saw the desert and the garden, mingling their bloom and desolation together. I saw the love-bower and the tomb standing side by side, and pleasure and death keeping hourly watch upon each other. In the very luxury of the climate there was the same saddening influence. The monotonous splendour of the days, the solemn radiance of the nights—all tended to cherish that ardent melancholy, the offspring of passion and of thought, which had so long been the inmate of my soul. [34]

When I sailed from Alexandria, the inundation of the Nile was at its full. The whole valley of Egypt lay covered by its flood; and, as I saw around me, in the light of the setting sun, shrines, palaces, and monuments, encircled by the waters, I could almost fancy that I beheld the sinking island of Atalantis, on the last evening its temples were visible above the wave. Such varieties, too, of animation as presented themselves on every side!—

> While, far as sight can reach, beneath as clear
> And blue a heaven as ever bless'd this sphere,
> Gardens, and pillar'd streets, and porphyry domes,
> And high-built temples, fit to be the homes
> Of mighty gods, and pyramids, whose hour
> Outlasts all time, above the waters tower!

Then, too, the scenes of pomp and joy, that make
One theatre of this vast, peopled lake,
Where all that Love, Religion, Commerce gives
Of life and motion, ever moves and lives.
Here, up the steps of temples, from the wave
Ascending, in procession slow and grave,
Priests, in white garments, go, with sacred wands
[35]   And silver cymbals gleaming in their hands:
While, there, rich barks—fresh from those sunny tracts
Far off, beyond the sounding cataracts—
Glide with their precious lading to the sea,
Plumes of bright birds, rhinoceros' ivory,
Gems from the isle of Meröe, and those grains
Of gold, wash'd down by Abyssinian rains.

Here, where the waters wind into a bay
Shadowy and cool, some pilgrims, on their way
To Saïs or Bubastus, among beds
Of lotus-flowers, that close above their heads,
Push their light barks, and hid, as in a bower,
Sing, talk, or sleep away the sultry hour;
While haply, not far off, beneath a bank
Of blossoming acacias, many a prank
Is play'd in the cool current by a train
Of laughing nymphs, lovely as she, whose chain
Around two conquerors of the world was cast,
But, for a third too feeble, broke at last!

Enchanted with the whole scene, I lingered on my voyage,
visiting all those luxurious and venerable places, whose names
have been consecrated by the wonder of ages. At Saïs I was
present during her Festival of Lamps, and read, by the blaze of
[36]   innumerable lights, those sublime words on the temple of Neitha:
"I am all that has been, that is, and that will be, and no man hath
ever lifted my veil." I wandered among the prostrate obelisks of

Heliopolis, and saw, not without a sigh, the sun smiling over her ruins, as if in mockery of the mass of perishable grandeur, that had once called itself, in its pride, "The City of the Sun." But to the Isle of the Golden Venus was my fondest pilgrimage;—and as I explored its shades, where bowers are the only temples, I felt how far more fit to form the shrine of a Deity are the ever-living stems of the garden and the grove, than the most precious columns that the inanimate quarry can supply.

Every where new pleasures, new interests awaited me; and though Melancholy, as usual, stood always near, her shadow fell but half-way over my vagrant path, and left the rest more welcomely brilliant from the contrast. To relate my various adventures, during this short voyage, would only detain me from events, far, far more worthy of record. Amidst such endless [37] variety of attractions, the great object of my journey was forgotten;—the mysteries of this land of the sun were, to me, as much mysteries as ever, and I had as yet been initiated in nothing but its pleasures.

It was not till that evening, when I first stood before the Pyramids of Memphis, and saw them towering aloft, like the watch-towers of Time, from whose summit, when he expires, he will look his last,—it was not till this moment that the great secret, of which I had dreamed, again rose, in all its inscrutable darkness, upon my thoughts. There was a solemnity in the sunshine that rested upon those monuments—a stillness, as of reverence, in the air around them, that stole, like the music of past times, into my heart. I thought what myriads of the wise, the beautiful, and the brave, had sunk into dust since earth first beheld those wonders; and, in the sadness of my soul, I exclaimed,—"Must man alone, then, perish? must minds and hearts be annihilated, [38] while pyramids endure? Death, Death, even on these everlasting tablets,—the only approach to immortality that kings themselves could purchase,—thou hast written our doom, saying, awfully and intelligibly, 'There is, for man, no eternal mansion, but the tomb!' "

My heart sunk at the thought; and, for the moment, I yielded to that desolate feeling, which overspreads the soul that hath no light from the future. But again the buoyancy of my nature prevailed, and again, the willing dupe of vain dreams, I deluded myself into the belief of all that I most wished, with that happy facility which makes imagination stand in place of happiness. "Yes," I cried, "immortality *must* be within man's reach; and, as wisdom alone is worthy of such a blessing, to the wise alone must the secret have been revealed. Deep, it is said, under yonder pyramid, has for ages lain concealed the Table of Emerald, on which the Thrice-Great Hermes engraved, before the flood, the secret of Alchemy, that gives gold at will. Why may not the mightier, the more god-like secret, that gives life at will, be recorded there also? It was by the power of gold, of endless gold, that the kings, who repose in those massy structures, scooped earth to the centre, and raised quarries into the air, to provide themselves with tombs that might outstand the world. Who can tell but that the gift of immortality was also theirs? who knows but that they themselves, triumphant over decay, still live—those mansions, which we call tombs, being rich and everlasting palaces, within whose depths, concealed from this withering world, they still wander, with the few who are sharers of their gift, through a sunless, but illuminated, elysium of their own? Else, wherefore those structures? wherefore that subterraneous realm, by which the whole valley of Egypt is undermined? Why, else, those labyrinths, which none of earth hath ever beheld—which none of heaven, except that God, with the finger on his hushed lip, hath trodden!"

While I indulged in these dreams, the sun, half sunk beneath the horizon, was taking, calmly and gloriously, his leave of the Pyramids,—as he had done, evening after evening, for ages, till they had become familiar to him as the earth itself. On the side turned to his ray they now presented a front of dazzling whiteness, while, on the other, their great shadows, lengthening to the eastward, looked like the first steps of Night, hastening to envelope the hills of Araby in her shade.

No sooner had the last gleam of the sun disappeared, than, on every house-top in Memphis, gay, gilded banners were seen waving aloft, to proclaim his setting,—while a full burst of harmony pealed from all the temples along the shores.

Startled from my musing by these sounds, I at once recollected, that, on that very evening, the great festival of the Moon was [41] to be celebrated. On a little island, half-way over between the gardens of Memphis and the eastern shore, stood the temple of that goddess,

> Whose beams
> Bring the sweet time of night-flowers and dreams.
> *Not* the cold Dian of the North, who chains
> In vestal ice the current of young veins;
> But she, who haunts the gay, Bubastian grove,
> And owns she sees, from her bright heav'n above,
> Nothing on earth, to match that heav'n, but love!

Thus did I exclaim, in the words of one of their own Egyptian poets, as, anticipating the various delights of the festival, I cast away from my mind all gloomy thoughts, and, hastening to my little bark, in which I now lived, like a Nile-bird, on the waters, steered my course to the island-temple of the Moon.

CHAP. V.

The rising of the Moon, slow and majestic, as if conscious of the honours that awaited her upon earth, was welcomed with a loud acclaim from every eminence, where multitudes stood watching for her first light. And seldom had she risen upon a scene more beautiful. Memphis,—still grand, though no longer the unrivalled Memphis, that had borne away from Thebes the crown of supremacy, and worn it undisputed through so many centuries,—now, softened by the moonlight that harmonised with her decline, shone forth among her lakes, her pyramids, and her shrines, like a dream of glory that was soon to pass away. Ruin, even now, was but too visible around her. The sands of the Libyan desert gained upon her like a sea; and, among solitary columns and sphinxes, already half sunk from sight, Time seemed to stand waiting, till all, that now flourished around, should fall beneath his desolating hand, like the rest.

On the waters all was life and gaiety. As far as eye could reach, the lights of innumerable boats were seen, studding, like rubies, the surface of the stream. Vessels of all kinds,—from the light coracle, built for shooting down the cataracts, to the large yacht that glides to the sound of flutes,—all were afloat for this sacred festival, filled with crowds of the young and the gay, not only from Memphis and Babylon, but from cities still farther removed from the scene.

As I approached the island, I could see, glittering through the trees on the bank, the lamps of the pilgrims hastening to the ceremony. Landing in the direction which those lights pointed out, I soon joined the crowd; and, passing through a long

alley of sphinxes, whose spangling marble shone out from the
dark sycamores around them, in a short time reached the grand   [44]
vestibule of the temple, where I found the ceremonies of the
evening already commenced.

In this vast hall, which was surrounded by a double range of
columns, and lay open over-head to the stars of heaven, I saw
a group of young maidens, moving in a sort of measured step,
between walk and dance, round a small shrine, upon which stood
one of those sacred birds, that, on account of the variegated
colour of their wings, are dedicated to the moon. The vestibule
was dimly lighted,—there being but one lamp of naptha on each
of the great pillars that encircled it. But, having taken my station
beside one of those pillars, I had a distinct view of the young
dancers, as in succession they passed me.

Their long, graceful drapery was as white as snow; and each
wore loosely, beneath the rounded bosom, a dark-blue zone, or
bandelet, studded, like the skies at midnight, with little silver
stars. Through their dark locks was wreathed the white lily of   [45]
the Nile,—that flower being accounted as welcome to the moon,
as the golden blossoms of the bean-flower are to the sun. As
they passed under the lamp, a gleam of light flashed from their
bosoms, which, I could perceive, was the reflection of a small
mirror, that, in the manner of the women of the East, each wore
beneath her left shoulder.

There was no music to regulate their steps; but, as they gracefully went round the bird on the shrine, some, by the beat of the
castanet, some, by the shrill ring of the sistrum,—which they held
uplifted in the attitude of their own divine Isis,—harmoniously
timed the cadence of their feet; while others, at every step, shook
a small chain of silver, whose sound, mingling with those of the
castanets and sistrums, produced a wild, but not an unpleasing
harmony.

They seemed all lovely; but there was one—whose face the
light had not yet reached, so downcast she held it,—who attract-   [46]

ed, and, at length, riveted all my attention. I knew not why, but there was a something in those half-seen features,—a charm in the very shadow, that hung over their imagined beauty,—which took me more than all the out-shining loveliness of her companions. So enchained was my fancy by this coy mystery, that her alone, of all the group, could I either see or think of—her alone I watched, as, with the same downcast brow, she glided round the altar, gently and aërially, as if her presence, like that of a spirit, was something to be felt, not seen.

Suddenly, while I gazed, the loud crash of a thousand cymbals was heard;—the massy gates of the Temple flew open, as if by magic, and a flood of radiance from the illuminated aisle filled the whole vestibule; while, at the same instant, as if the light and the sounds were born together, a peal of rich harmony came mingling with the radiance.

[47]   It was then,—by that light, which shone full upon the young maiden's features, as, starting at the blaze, she raised her eyes to the portal, and, as suddenly, let fall their lids again,—it was then I beheld, what even my own ardent imagination, in its most vivid dreams of beauty, had never pictured. Not Psyche herself, when pausing on the threshold of heaven, while its first glories fell on her dazzled lids, could have looked more beautiful, or blushed with a more innocent shame. Often as I had felt the power of looks, none had ever entered into my soul so far. It was a new feeling—a new sense—coming as suddenly as that radiance into the vestibule, and, at once, filling my whole being;—and had that vision but lingered another moment before my eyes, I should have wholly forgotten who I was and where, and thrown myself, in prostrate adoration, at her feet.

But scarcely had that gush of harmony been heard, when the sacred bird, which had, till now, stood motionless as an image, [48]   expanded his wings, and flew into the Temple; while his graceful young worshippers, with a fleetness like his own, followed,—and she, who had left a dream in my heart never to be forgotten, vanished with the rest. As she went rapidly past the pillar against which I leaned, the ivy that encircled it caught in her drapery, and disengaged some ornament which fell to the ground. It was the small mirror which I had seen shining on her bosom. Hastily and tremulously I picked it up, and hurried to restore it;—but she was already lost to my eyes in the crowd.

In vain I tried to follow;—the aisles were already filled, and numbers of eager pilgrims pressed towards the portal. But the servants of the Temple prevented all further entrance, and still, as I presented myself, their white wands barred the way. Perplexed and irritated amid that crowd of faces, regarding all as enemies that impeded my progress, I stood on tiptoe, gazing into the busy aisles, and with a heart beating as I caught, from time to time, a [49] glimpse of some spangled zone, or lotus wreath, which led me to fancy that I had discovered the object of my search. But it was all in vain;—in every direction, files of sacred nymphs were moving, but nowhere could I see her, whom alone I sought.

In this state of breathless agitation did I stand for some time,—bewildered with the confusion of faces and lights, as well as with the clouds of incense that rolled around me,—till, fevered and impatient, I could endure it no longer. Forcing my way out of the vestibule into the cool air, I hurried back through the alley of sphinxes to the shore, and flung myself into my boat.

There is, to the north of Memphis, a solitary lake (which, at this season of the year, mingles with the rest of the waters,) upon whose shores stands the Necropolis, or City of the Dead—a place of melancholy grandeur, covered over with shrines and pyramids, where many a kingly head, proud even in death, has [50] for ages awaited the resurrection of its glories. Through a range of sepulchral grots underneath, the humbler denizens of the tomb are deposited,—looking out on each successive generation that visits them, with the same face and features they wore centuries ago. Every plant and tree, that is consecrated to death, from the asphodel-flower to the mystic plantain, lends its sweetness or shadow to this place of tombs; and the only noise that disturbs its eternal calm, is the low humming sound of the priests at prayer, when a new inhabitant is added to the silent city.

It was towards this place of death that, in a mood of mind, as usual, half bright, half gloomy, I now, almost unconsciously, directed my bark. The form of the young Priestess was continually before me. That one bright look of hers, the very memory of which was worth all the actual smiles of others, never left my mind. Absorbed in such thoughts, I rowed on, scarce knowing [51] whither I went, till, startled by finding myself within the shadow of the City of the Dead, I looked up, and saw, rising in succession before me, pyramid beyond pyramid, each towering more loftily than the other,—while all were out-topped in grandeur by one, upon whose summit the moon seemed to rest, as on a pedestal.

Drawing near to the shore, which was sufficiently elevated to raise this city of monuments above the level of the inundation, I lifted my oar, and let the boat rock idly on the water, while my thoughts, left equally without direction, fluctuated as idly. How various and vague were the dreams that then passed through my mind—that bright vision of the temple mingling itself with all! Sometimes she stood before me, like an aërial spirit, as pure as if that element of music and light, into which I had seen her vanish, was her only dwelling. Sometimes, animated with passion, and kindling into a creature of earth, she seemed to lean towards me [52] with looks of tenderness, which it were worth worlds, but for one instant, to inspire; and again—as the dark fancies, that ever haunted me, recurred—I saw her cold, parched, and blackening, amid the gloom of those eternal sepulchres before me!

Turning away, with a shudder, from the cemetery at this thought, I heard the sound of an oar plying swiftly through the water, and, in a few moments, saw, shooting past me towards the shore, a small boat in which sat two female figures, muffled up and veiled. Having landed them not far from the spot where I lay,—concealed by the shadow of a monument on the bank,—the boat again departed, with the same fleetness, over the flood.

Never had the prospect of an adventure come more welcome than at this moment, when my fancy was weaving such chains for my heart, as threatened a bondage, of all others, the most difficult to break. To become enamoured thus of a creature of my own imagination, was the worst, because the most lasting, of [53] follies. Reality alone gives a chance of dissolving such spells, and the idol I was now creating to myself must for ever remain ideal. Any pursuit, therefore, that seemed likely to divert me from such thoughts—to bring back my imagination to earth and reality, from the vague region in which it was wandering, was a relief too seasonable not to be welcomed with eagerness.

I had watched the course which the two figures took, and, having hastily fastened my boat to the bank, stepped gently on shore, and, at a little distance, followed them. The windings through which they led were intricate; but, by the bright light of the moon, I was enabled to keep their forms in view, as, with rapid step, they glided among the monuments. At length, in the shade of a small pyramid, whose peak barely surmounted the plane-trees that grew nigh, they vanished from my sight. I hastened to the spot, but there was not a sign of life around; and had my creed [54] extended to another world, I might have fancied that these forms were spirits, sent from thence to mock me,—so instantaneously they disappeared. I searched through the neighbouring grove, but all there was still as death. At length, in examining one of the sides of the pyramid, which, for a few feet from the ground, was furnished with steps, I found, midway between peak and base, a part of the surface, which, though presenting an appearance of smoothness to the eye, gave to the touch, I thought, indications of a concealed opening.

After a variety of efforts and experiments, I, at last, more by accident than skill, pressed the spring that commanded this mysterious aperture. In an instant the portal slid aside, and disclosed a narrow stair-way within, the two or three first steps of which

[55]

were discernible by the moonlight, while the rest were lost in utter darkness. Though it was difficult to conceive that the persons whom I had followed would have ventured to pass through this gloomy opening, yet to account for their disappearance otherwise was still more difficult. At all events, my curiosity was now too eager in the chase to relinquish it;—the spirit of adventure, once raised, could not be so easily laid. Accordingly, having sent up a gay prayer to that bliss-loving Queen whose eye alone was upon me, I passed through the portal and descended into the pyramid.

CHAP. VI.

At the bottom of the stair-way I found myself in a low, narrow passage, through which, without stooping almost to earth, it was impossible to proceed. Though leading through a multiplicity of dark windings, this way seemed but little to advance my progress,—its course, I perceived, being chiefly circular, and gathering, at every turn, but a deeper intensity of darkness.

"Can this," I thought, "be the sojourn of any thing human?"—and had scarcely asked myself the question, when the path opened into a long gallery, at the farthest end of which a gleam of light was visible. This welcome glimmer appeared to come from some cell or alcove, in which the right-hand wall of the gallery terminated, and, breathless with expectation, I stole gently towards it.

Arrived at the end of the gallery, a scene presented itself to my eyes, for which my fondest expectations of adventure could not have prepared me. The place from which the light proceeded was a small chapel, of whose interior, from the dark recess in which I stood, I had, unseen myself, a full and distinct view. Over the walls of this oratory were painted some of those various symbols, by which the mystic wisdom of the Egyptians loves to shadow out the History of the Soul—the winged globe with a serpent,—the rays descending from above, like a glory, and the Theban beetle, as he comes forth, after the waters have passed away, and the first sunbeam falls on his regenerated wings.

In the middle of the chapel stood a low altar of granite, on which lay a lifeless female form, enshrined within a case of crystal,—as they preserve their dead in Ethiopia,—and looking as freshly beautiful as if the soul had but a few hours departed. Among the emblems of death, on the front of the altar, were a slender lotus-branch, broken in two, and a bird, just winging its flight from the spray.

To these memorials of the dead, however, I but little attended; for there was a living object there upon which my eyes were most intently fixed.

The lamp, by which the whole of the chapel was illuminated, was placed at the head of the pale image in the shrine; and, between its light and me, stood a female form, bending over the monument, as if to gaze upon the silent features within. The position in which this figure was placed, intercepting a strong light, afforded me, at first, but an imperfect and shadowy view of it. Yet even at this mere outline my heart beat high,—and memory, as it proved, had as much share in this feeling as imagination. For, on the head changing its position, so as to let a gleam fall on the features, I saw with a transport, which had almost led me to betray my lurking-place, that it was she—the young worshipper of Isis—the same, the very same, whom I had seen, brightening the holy place where she stood, and looking like an inhabitant of some purer world.

The movement, by which she had now given me an opportunity of recognising her, was made in raising from the shrine a small cross[2] of silver, which lay directly over the bosom of the lifeless figure. Bringing it close to her lips, she kissed it with a religious fervour; then, turning her eyes mournfully upwards, held them fixed with an inspired earnestness, as if, at that moment, in direct communion with heaven, they saw neither roof, nor any other earthly barrier between them and the skies.

What a power hath innocence, whose very helplessness is its safeguard—in whose presence even Passion himself stands

---

[2] A cross was, among the Egyptians, the emblem of a future life.

[58]

[59]

[60]

abashed, and turns worshipper at the altar which he came to despoil. She, who, but a short hour before, had presented herself to my imagination, as something I could have risked immortality to win—she, whom gladly, from the floor of her own lighted temple, in the very face of its proud ministers, I would have borne away in triumph, and defied all punishments, both human and sacred, to make her mine,—she was now before me, thrown, as if by fate itself, into my power—standing there, beautiful and alone, with nothing but her innocence for her guard! Yet, no—so touching was the purity of the whole scene, so calm and august that protection which the dead seemed to extend over the living, that every earthlier feeling was forgotten as I gazed, and love itself became exalted into reverence.

Entranced, indeed, as I felt in witnessing such a scene, thus to enjoy it by stealth, seemed a wrong, a sacrilege—and, rather than let her eyes meet the flash of mine, or disturb, by a whisper, [61] that sacred silence, in which Youth and Death held communion through Love, I would have let my heart break, without a murmur, where I stood. Gently, as if life depended upon every movement, I stole away from that tranquil and holy scene—leaving it still tranquil and holy as I found it—and, gliding back through the same passages and windings by which I had entered, regained the narrow stair-way, and again ascended into light.

The sun had just risen, and, from the summit of the Arabian hills, was pouring down his beams into that vast valley of waters,—as if proud of the homage that had been paid to his own Isis, now fading away in the superior light of her Lord. My first impulse was to fly from this dangerous spot, and in new loves and pleasures seek forgetfulness of the scene which I had witnessed. "Once out of the circle of this enchantment," I [62] exclaimed, "I know my own susceptibility to new impressions too well, to doubt that I shall soon break the spell that is around me."

But vain were my efforts and resolves. Even while I swore

to fly, my steps were still lingering round the pyramid—my eyes still turned towards the secret portal, which severed this enchantress from the world of the living. Hour after hour did I wander through that City of Silence,—till, already, it was noon, and, under the sun's meridian eye, the mighty pyramid of pyramids stood, like a great spirit, shadowless.

Again did those wild and passionate feelings, which had, for a moment, been subdued into reverence by her presence, return to kindle up my imagination and senses. I even reproached myself for the awe, that had held me spell-bound before her. "What would my companions of the Garden say, did they know that their chief,—he, whose path Love had strewed with trophies—was now pining for a simple Egyptian girl, in whose presence he had not dared to give utterance to a sigh, and who had vanquished the victor, without even knowing her triumph!"

[63]

A blush came over my cheek at the humiliating thought, and my determination was fixed to await her coming. That she should be an inmate of those gloomy caverns seemed inconceivable; nor did there appear to be any issue from their depths but by the pyramid. Again, therefore, like a sentinel of the dead, did I pace up and down among these tombs, contrasting, in many a mournful reflection, the burning fever within my own veins with the cold quiet of those who slept around.

At length the fierce glow of the sun over my head, and, still more, that ever restless agitation in my heart, were too much for even strength like mine to bear. Exhausted, I lay down at the base of the pyramid—placing myself directly under the portal, where, even should slumber surprise me, my heart, if not my ear, might still be on the watch, and her footstep, light as it was, could not fail to awake me.

[64]

After many an ineffectual struggle against drowsiness, I at length sunk into sleep—but not into forgetfulness. The same image still haunted me, in every variety of shape, with which imagination, assisted by memory, could invest it. Now, like

Neïtha, upon her throne at Saïs, she seemed to sit, with the veil just raised from that brow, which mortal had never, till then, beheld,—and now, like the beautiful enchantress Rhodope, I saw her rise out of the pyramid in which she had dwelt for ages,—

"Fair Rhodope, as story tells,
The bright, unearthly nymph, who dwells
Mid sunless gold and jewels hid,
The Lady of the Pyramid!"

So long, amid that unbroken silence, did my sleep continue, that I found the moon again shining above the horizon, when I [65] awoke. All around was silent and lifeless as before, nor did a print upon the herbage betray that any foot had passed it since my own. Refreshed by rest, and with a fancy still more excited by the mystic wonders of which I had been dreaming, I now resolved to revisit the chapel in the pyramid, and put an end, if possible, to this illusion that haunted me.

Having learned from the experience of the preceding night, the inconvenience of encountering those labyrinths without a light, I now hastened to provide myself with a lamp from my boat. Tracking my way back with some difficulty to the shore, I there found, not only my lamp, but some dates and dried fruits, with a store of which, for my roving life upon the waters, I was always supplied,—and which now, after so many hours of abstinence, were a welcome and necessary relief.

Thus prepared, I again ascended the pyramid, and was pro- ceeding to search out the secret spring, when a loud, dismal [66] noise was heard at a distance, to which all the echoes of the cemetery answered. It came, I knew, from the Great Temple on the shore of the Lake, and was the shriek which its gates—the Gates of Oblivion, as they were called—sent forth from their hinges, in opening at night, to receive within their precincts the newly-landed dead.

I had heard that sound before, and always with sadness; but, at this moment, it thrilled through me, like a voice of ill omen, and I almost doubted whether I should not abandon my enterprise. The hesitation, however, was but momentary;—even while it passed through my mind, I had touched the spring of the portal. In a few seconds more, I was again in the passage beneath the pyramid, and being enabled by my lamp to follow the windings of the way more rapidly, soon found myself at the door of the small chapel in the gallery.

[67]

I entered, still awed, though there was now nothing living within. The young Priestess had fled—had vanished, like a spirit, into the darkness. All the rest was as I had left it on the preceding night. The lamp still stood burning upon the crystal shrine—the cross lay where the hands of the young mourner had placed it, and the cold image beneath wore the same tranquil look, as if resigned to the solitude of death—of all lone things the loneliest. Remembering the lips that I had seen kiss that cross, and kindling with the recollection, I raised it passionately to my own;—but, at the same moment, I fancied the dead eyes met mine, and, saddened in the midst of my ardour, I replaced the cross upon the shrine.

I had now lost all clue to the object of my pursuit, and was preparing slowly to retrace my steps to earth, with that gloomy satisfaction which certainty, even when unwelcome, brings,—when, as I held forth my lamp, on leaving the chapel, I could perceive that the gallery, instead of terminating here, took a sudden bend to the left, which had before eluded my eye, and which gave a promise of leading still further into those recesses. Re-animated by this discovery, which opened a new source of hope to my heart, I cast but one hesitating look at my lamp, as if to ask whether it would be faithful through the gloom I was about to encounter, and, without further thought, rushed eagerly forward.

[68]

CHAP. VII.

The path led, for some time, through the same sort of narrow windings as those which I had encountered in descending the stair-way; and at length opened, in a similar manner, into a straight and steep gallery, along each side of which stood, closely ranged and upright, a file of lifeless bodies, whose glassy eyes threw a preternatural glare upon me as I passed.

Arrived at the end of this gallery, I found my hopes a second time vanish. The path, I perceived, extended no further. The only object that I could discern, by the glimmering of my lamp, which now, every minute, burned fainter and fainter, was the mouth of a huge well, that lay gaping before me—a reservoir of darkness, black and unfathomable. It now crossed my memory that I had heard of such wells, as being used occasionally for passages by the Priests. Leaning down, therefore, over the edge, [70] I looked anxiously within, to discover whether it was possible to descend into the chasm; but the sides were hard and smooth as glass, being varnished all over with that dark pitch, which the Dead Sea throws out on its slimy shore.

After a more attentive scrutiny, however, I observed, at the depth of a few feet, a sort of iron step, projecting dimly from the side, and, below it, another, which, though hardly perceptible, was just sufficient to encourage an adventurous foot to the trial. Though all hope of tracing the young Priestess was at an end,—it being impossible that female foot should have dared this descent,—yet, as I had so far engaged in the adventure, and there was, at least, a mystery to be unravelled, I determined, at all hazards, to explore the chasm. Placing my lamp (which was hollowed at the bottom, so as to fit like a helmet) firmly on my head, and having thus both hands at liberty for exertion, I set my foot cautiously on the iron step, and descended into the well.

I found the same footing, at regular intervals, to a considerable depth; and had already counted near a hundred of these steps, when the ladder altogether ceased, and I could descend no farther. In vain did I stretch down my foot in search of support—the hard, slippery sides were all that it encountered. At length, stooping my head, so as to let the light fall below, I observed an opening or window directly above the step on which I stood, and, taking for granted that the way must lie in that direction, with some little difficulty clambered through the aperture.

I now found myself on a rude and narrow stair-way, the steps of which were cut out of the living rock, and wound spirally downward in the same direction as the well. Almost dizzy with the descent, which seemed as if it would never end, I, at last, reached the bottom, where a pair of massy iron gates closed directly across my path, as if to forbid any further progress. Massy, however, and gigantic as they were, I found, to my surprise, that the hand of an infant might have opened them with ease—so readily did their great folds give way to my touch,

> "Light as a lime-bush, that receives
> Some wandering bird among its leaves."

No sooner, however, had I passed through, than the din, with which the gates clashed together again, was such as might have awakened death itself. It seemed as if every echo, throughout that vast, subterranean world, from the Catacombs of Alexandria to Thebes's Valley of Kings, had caught up and repeated the thundering sound.

Startled, however, as I was, not even this supernatural clangour could divert my attention from the light that now broke upon me—soft, warm, and welcome as are the stars of his own

[71]

[72]

South to the mariner who has been wandering through the seas [73] of the north. Looking for the source of this splendour, I saw, through an archway opposite, a long illuminated alley, stretching away as far as the eye could reach, and fenced, on one side, with thickets of odoriferous shrubs, while, along the other, extended a line of lofty arcades, from which the light, that filled the whole area, issued. As soon, too, as the din of the deep echoes had subsided, there stole gradually on my ear a strain of choral music, which appeared to come, mellowed and sweetened in its passage, through many a spacious hall within those shining arcades. Among the voices I could distinguish some female tones, towering high and clear over all the rest, and forming the spire, as it were, into which the harmony tapered, as it rose.

So excited was my fancy by this sudden enchantment, that—though never had I caught a sound from the young Egyptian's lips,—I yet persuaded myself that the voice I now heard [74] was hers, sounding highest and most heavenly of all that choir, and calling to me, like a distant spirit out of its sphere. Animated by this thought, I flew forward to the archway, but found, to my mortification, that it was guarded by a trellis-work, whose bars, though invisible at a distance, resisted all my efforts to force them.

While occupied in these ineffectual struggles, I perceived, to the left of the archway, a dark, cavernous opening, which seemed to lead in a direction parallel to the lighted arcades. Notwithstanding my impatience, however, the aspect of this passage, as I looked shudderingly into it, chilled my very blood. It was not so much darkness, as a sort of livid and ghastly twilight, from which a damp, like that of death-vaults, exhaled, and through which, if my eyes did not deceive me, pale, phantom-like shapes were, at that very moment, hovering. [75]

Looking anxiously round, to discover some less formidable outlet, I saw, over the vast folding-gates through which I had just passed, a blue, tremulous flame, which, after playing for a few

seconds over the dark ground of the pediment, settled gradually
into characters of light, and formed the following words:—

You, who would try
   Yon terrible track,
To live, or to die,
   But ne'er to look back—

You, who aspire
   To be purified there,
By the terrors of Fire,
   Of Water, and Air,—

If danger, and pain,
   And death you despise,
On—for again
   Into light you shall rise;

Rise into light
   With that Secret Divine,
Now shrouded from sight
   By the Veils of the Shrine!

But if——

Here the letters faded away into a dead blank, more awfully intelligible than the most eloquent words.

A new hope now flashed across me. The dream of the Garden, which had been for some time almost forgotten, returned to my mind. "Am I then," I exclaimed, "in the path to the promised mystery? and shall the great secret of Eternal Life *indeed* be mine?"

"Yes!" seemed to answer, out of the air, that spirit-voice, which still was heard crowning the choir with its single sweetness. I hailed the omen with transport. Love and Immortality, both beckoning me onward—who could give a thought to fear, with two such bright hopes in view? Having invoked and blessed that unknown enchantress, whose steps had led me to this abode of mystery and knowledge, I plunged into the chasm.

Instead of that vague, spectral twilight which had at first met my eye, I now found, as I entered, a thick darkness, which, though [77] far less horrible, was, at this moment, still more disconcerting, as my lamp, which had been, for some time, almost useless, was fast expiring. Resolved, however, to make the most of its last gleam, I hastened, with rapid step, through this gloomy region, which seemed wider and more open to the air than any that I had yet passed. Nor was it long before the appearance of a bright blaze in the distance announced to me that my first great Trial was at hand. As I drew nearer, the flames burst high and wide on all sides;—and the spectacle that now presented itself was such as might have appalled even hearts more habituated to dangers than mine.

There lay before me, extending completely across my path, a thicket, or grove of the most combustible trees of Egypt—tamarind, pine, and Arabian balm. Around their stems and branches were coiled serpents of fire, which, twisting them- [78] selves rapidly from bough to bough, spread their own wild-fire as they went, and involved tree after tree in one general blaze. It was, indeed, rapid as the burning of those reed-beds of Ethiopia, whose light brightens, at night, the distant cataracts of the Nile.

Through the middle of this blazing grove, I perceived, my only pathway lay. There was not a moment to be lost—the conflagration gained rapidly on either side, and already the narrowing path between was strewed with fire. Casting away my now useless lamp, and holding my robe as some protection over my head, with a tremor, I own, in every limb, I ventured through the blaze.

Instantly, as if my presence had given new life to the flames, a fresh outbreak of combustion arose on all sides. The trees clustered into a bower of fire above my head, while the serpents, that hung hissing from the red branches, shot showers of sparkles down upon me, as I passed. Never were decision and activity more serviceable;—one minute later, and I must have perished. The narrow opening, of which I had so promptly availed myself, closed instantly behind me; and, as I looked back, to contemplate the ordeal which I had passed, I saw that the whole grove was already one mass of fire.

Happy at having escaped this first trial, I plucked from one of the pine-trees a bough that was but just kindled, and, with this for my only guide, hastened breathlessly forward. I had gone but a few paces, when the path turned suddenly off,—leading downwards, as I could see by the glimmer of my brand, into a more confined space, through which a chilling air, as if from some neighbouring waters, blew over my brow. Nor had I proceeded very far, when the sound of torrents fell on my ear,—mingled, as I thought, from time to time, with shrill wailings, like the cries of persons in danger or distress. At every step the noise of the dashing waters increased, and I now perceived that I had entered an immense rocky cavern, through the middle of which, headlong as a winter-torrent, the flood, to whose roar I had been listening, rushed. Upon its surface, too, there floated strange, spectre-like shapes, which, as they went by, sent forth those dismal shrieks, as if in fear of some precipice to whose brink they were hurrying.

I saw too plainly that my course must be across that torrent. It was fearful; but in courage lay my only hope. What awaited me on the opposite shore, I knew not; for all there was wrapped in impenetrable gloom, nor could the weak light I held reach half so far. Dismissing, however, all thoughts but that of pressing onward, I sprung from the rock on which I stood into the flood,—trusting that, with my right hand, I should be able to buffet the current, while, with the other, I might contrive to hold my brand aloft, as long as a glimmer of it remained, to guide me [81] to the shore.

Long and formidable was the struggle I had to maintain. More than once, overpowered by the rush of the waters, I had almost given myself up, as destined to follow those apparitions, that still passed me, hurrying, with mournful cries, to their doom in some invisible gulf before them.

At length, just as my strength was nearly exhausted, and the last remains of the pine-branch were falling from my hand, I saw, outstretching towards me into the water, a light double balustrade, with a flight of steps between, ascending, almost perpendicularly, from the wave, till they seemed lost in a dense mass of clouds above. This glimpse—for it was no more, as my light expired in giving it—lent new spring to my courage. Having now both hands at liberty, so desperate were my efforts, that after a few minutes' struggle, I felt my brow strike against [82] the stairway, and, in an instant more, my feet were on the steps.

Rejoiced at my rescue from that perilous flood, though I knew not whither the stairway led, I promptly ascended it. But this feeling of confidence was of short duration. I had not mounted far, when, to my horror, I perceived, that each successive step, as my foot left it, broke away from beneath me,—leaving me in midair, with no other alternative than that of mounting still by the same momentary footing, and with the dreadful doubt whether it would even endure my tread.

And thus did I, for a few seconds, continue to ascend, with

nothing beneath me but that awful river, in which—so tranquil it had become—I could hear the plash of the falling fragments, as every step in succession gave way under my feet. It was a trying moment, but still worse remained. I now found the balustrade, by which I had held during my ascent, and which had hitherto seemed firm, grow tremulous in my hand,—while the step to which I was about to trust myself, tottered under my foot. Just then, a momentary flash, as if of lightning, broke around, and I saw, hanging out of the clouds, within my reach, a huge brazen ring. Instinctively I stretched forth my arm to seize it, and, at the same instant, both balustrade and steps gave way beneath me, and I was left swinging by my hands in the dark void. As if, too, this massy ring, which I grasped, was by some magic power linked with all the winds in heaven, no sooner had I seized it than, like the touching of a spring, it seemed to give loose to every variety of gusts and tempests, that ever strewed the sea-shore with wrecks or dead; and, as I swung about, the sport of this elemental strife, each new burst of its fury threatened to shiver me, like a storm-sail, to atoms!

[83]

Nor was even this the worst;—still holding, I know not how, by the ring, I felt myself caught up, as if by a thousand whirl-winds, and round and round, like a stone-shot in a sling, whirled in the midst of all this deafening chaos, till my brain grew dizzy, and my recollection confused, and I almost fancied myself on that wheel of the infernal world, whose rotations, it is said, Eternity alone can number!

[84]

Human strength could no longer sustain such a trial. I was on the point, at last, of loosing my hold, when suddenly the violence of the storm moderated;—my whirl through the air gradually ceased, and I felt the ring slowly descend with me, till—happy as a shipwrecked mariner at the first touch of land—I found my feet once more upon firm ground.

At the same moment, a light of the most delicious softness filled the whole air. Music, such as is heard in dreams, came floating at a distance; and, as my eyes gradually recovered their powers of vision, a scene of glory was revealed to them, almost too bright for imagination, and yet living and real. As far as the sight could reach, enchanting gardens were seen, opening [85] away through long tracts of light and verdure, and sparkling every where with fountains, that circulated, like streams of life, among the flowers. Not a charm was here wanting, that the imagination of poet or prophet, in their pictures of Elysium, ever yet dreamed or promised. Vistas, opening into scenes of indistinct grandeur,—streams, shining out at intervals, in their shadowy course,—and labyrinths of flowers, leading, by mysterious windings, to green, spacious glades, full of splendour and repose. Over all this, too, there fell a light, from some unseen source, resembling nothing that illumines our upper world—a sort of golden moonlight, mingling the warm radiance of day with the calm and melancholy lustre of night.

Nor were there wanting inhabitants for this sunless Paradise. Through all the bright gardens were wandering, with the serene air and step of happy spirits, groups both of young and old, of [86] venerable and of lovely forms, bearing, most of them, the Nile's white flowers on their heads, and branches of the eternal palm in their hands; while, over the verdant turf, fair children and maidens went dancing to aërial music, whose source was, like that of the light, invisible, but which filled the whole air with its mystic sweetness.

Exhausted as I was by the trials I had undergone, no sooner did I perceive those fair groups in the distance, than my weariness, both of frame and spirit, was forgotten. A thought crossed me that she, whom I sought, might be among them; and, notwithstanding the awe, with which that unearthly scene inspired me, I was about to fly, on the instant, to ascertain my hope. But in the act of making the effort, I felt my robe gently pulled, and turning, beheld an aged man before me, whom, by the sacred hue of his garb, I knew to be a Hierophant. Placing a

[87]

branch of the consecrated palm in my hand, he said, in a solemn voice, "Aspirant of the Mysteries, welcome!"—then, regarding me for a few seconds with grave attention, added, in a tone of courteousness and interest, "The victory over the body hath been gained!—Follow me, young Greek, to thy resting place."

I obeyed in silence,—and the Priest, turning away from this scene of splendour, into a secluded path, where the light faded away, as we advanced, conducted me to a small pavilion, by the side of a whispering stream, where the very spirit of slumber seemed to preside, and, pointing to a bed of dried poppy-leaves within it, left me to repose.

CHAP. VIII.

Though the sight of that splendid scene which opened upon me, like a momentary glimpse into another world, had, for an instant, re-animated my strength and spirit, so completely had fatigue overmastered my whole frame, that, even had the form of the young Priestess stood before me, my limbs would have sunk in the effort to reach her. No sooner had I fallen on my leafy couch, than sleep, like a sudden death, came over me; and I lay, for hours, in the deep, and motionless rest, which not even a shadow of life disturbs.

On awaking I saw, beside me, the same venerable personage, who had welcomed me to this subterranean world on the preceding night. At the foot of my couch stood a statue, of Grecian workmanship, representing a boy, with wings, seated gracefully on a lotus-flower, and having the forefinger of his right hand pressed to his lips. This action, together with the glory round his brows, denoted, as I already knew, the God of Silence and Light.

Impatient to know what further trials awaited me, I was about to speak, when the Priest exclaimed, anxiously, "Hush!"—and pointing to this statue at the foot of the couch, said—"Let the spell of that Spirit be on thy lips, young stranger, till the wisdom of thy instructors shall think fit to remove it. Not unaptly doth the same god preside over Silence and Light; since it is only out of the depth of contemplative silence, that the great light of the soul, Truth, arises!"

Little used to the language of dictation or instruction, I was now preparing to rise, when the priest again restrained me; and, at

the same moment, two boys, beautiful as the young Genii of the
stars, entered the pavilion. They were habited in long garments
of the purest white, and bore each a small golden chalice in his
hand. Advancing towards me, they stopped on opposite sides of
the couch, and one of them, presenting to me his chalice of gold,
said, in a tone between singing and speaking,—

> "Drink of this cup—Osiris sips
>   The same in his halls below;
> And the same he gives, to cool the lips
>   Of the Dead, who downward go.

> "Drink of this cup—the water within
>   Is fresh from Lethe's stream;
> 'Twill make the past with all its sin,
>   And all its pain and sorrows, seem
>   Like a long-forgotten dream!

> "The pleasure, whose charms
>   Are steep'd in woe;
> The knowledge, that harms
>   The soul to know;

> "The hope, that, bright
>   As the lake of the waste,
> Allures the sight,
>   But mocks the taste;

> "The love, that binds
>   Its innocent wreath,
> Where the serpent winds,
>   In venom, beneath;—

"All that, of evil or false, by thee
   Hath ever been known or seen,
Shall melt away in this cup, and be
   Forgot, as it never had been!"

Unwilling to throw a slight on this strange ceremony, I leaned forward, with all due gravity, and tasted the cup; which I had no sooner done than the young cup-bearer, on the other side, invited my attention, and, in his turn, presenting the chalice which he held, sung, with a voice still sweeter than that of his companion, the following strain:—

"Drink of this cup—when Isis led
   Her boy, of old, to the beaming sky,
She mingled a draught divine, and said—
   'Drink of this cup, thou'lt never die!'

"Thus do I say and sing to thee,
   Heir of that boundless heav'n on high,
Though frail, and fall'n, and lost thou be,
   Drink of this cup, thou'lt never die!"

[92]

Much as I had endeavoured to keep my philosophy on its guard, against the illusions with which, I knew, this region abounded, the young cup-bearer had here touched a spring of imagination, over which, as has been seen, my philosophy had but little controul. No sooner had the words, "thou shalt never die," struck on my ear, than the dream of the Garden came fully to my mind, and, starting half-way from the couch, I stretched forth my hands to the cup. Recollecting myself, however, and fearful of having betrayed to others a weakness only fit for my own secret indulgence, with an affected smile of indifference I sunk back again on my couch,—while the young minstrel, but little interrupted by my movement, still continued his strain, of which I heard but the concluding words:—

"And Memory, too, with her dreams shall come,
  Dreams of a former, happier day,
When Heaven was still the Spirit's home,
  And her wings had not yet fallen away;

[93]

"Glimpses of glory, ne'er forgot,
  That tell, like gleams on a sunset sea,
What once hath been, what now is not,
  But, oh, what again shall brightly be!"

Though the assurances of immortality, contained in these verses, would, at any other moment,—vain and visionary as I thought them,—have sent my fancy wandering into reveries of the future, the effort of self-control I had just made enabled me to hear them with indifference.

Having gone through the form of tasting this second cup, I again looked anxiously to the Hierophant, to ascertain whether I might be permitted to rise. His assent having been given, the young pages brought to my couch a robe and tunic, which, like their own, were of linen of the purest white; and having assisted to clothe me in this sacred garb, they then placed upon my head a chaplet of myrtle, in which the symbol of Initiation, a golden

[94]

grasshopper, was seen shining out from among the dark leaves.

Though sleep had done much to refresh my frame, something more was still wanting to restore its strength; and it was not without a smile at my own reveries I reflected, how much more welcome than the young page's cup of immortality was the un-pretending, but real, repast now set before me,—fresh fruits from the Isle of Gardens in the Nile, the delicate flesh of the desert antelope, and wine from the Vineyard of the Queens at Anthylla, fanned by one of the pages with a palm-leaf, to keep it cool.

Having done justice to these dainties, it was with pleasure I heard the proposal of the Priest, that we should now walk forth together, and meditate among the scenes without. I had not forgotten the elysium that welcomed me last night,—those enchanted gardens, that mysterious music, and light, and the fair forms I saw wandering about,—as if, in the very midst of happiness, still seeking it. The hope, which had then occurred to me, that, perhaps, among those sparkling groups, might be the [95] maiden I sought, now returned with increased strength. I had little doubt that my guide was about to lead to the same Elysian scene, and that the form, so fit to inhabit it, would again appear before my eyes.

But far different was the region to which he conducted me; nor could the whole world produce a scene more gloomy, or more strange. It had the appearance of a small, solitary valley, inclosed, on every side, by rocks, which seemed to rise, almost perpendicularly, to the very sky;—for it was, indeed, the blue sky that I saw shining between their summits, and whose light, dimmed and half lost, in its descent thus far, formed the melancholy daylight of this nether world.[3] Down the side of these rocky [96] walls fell a cataract, whose source was upon earth, and on whose waters, as they rolled glassily over the edge above, a gleam of radiance rested, that showed how brilliant was the sunshine they left. From thence, gradually darkening, and broken, in its long descent, by alternate chasms and projections, the stream fell, at last, in a pale and thin mist—the phantom of what it had been on earth—into a small lake that lay at the base of the rock to receive it.

Nothing could be more bleak and saddening than the appearance of this lake. The usual ornaments of the waters of Egypt were not wanting: the lotus here uplifted her silvery flowers, and the crimson flamingo floated over the tide. But they were, neither of them, the same as in the upper world;—the flower had exchanged its whiteness for a livid hue, and the wings of the bird

---

[3] "On s'étoit même avisé, depuis la première construction de ces demeures, de percer en plusieurs endroits jusqu'au haut les terres qui les couvroient; non pas, à la vérité, pour tirer un jour qui n'auroit jamais été suffisant, mais pour recevoir un air salutaire, &c."—*Sethos.*

[97]
hung heavy and colourless. Every thing wore the same half-living aspect; and the only sounds that disturbed the mournful stillness were the wailing cry of a heron among the sedges, and that din of the waters, in their midway struggle, above.

There was an unearthly sadness in the whole scene, of which no heart, however light, could resist the influence. Perceiving how I was affected by it, "Such scenes," said the Priest, "are best suited to that solemn complexion of mind, which becomes him who approaches the Great Secret of futurity. Behold,"—and, in saying thus, he pointed to the opening over our heads, through which I could perceive a star or two twinkling in the heavens, though the sun had but a short time passed his meridian,—"as from this gloomy depth we can see those stars, which are now invisible to the dwellers upon the bright earth, even so, to the sad and self-humbled spirit, doth many a mystery of heaven reveal itself, of which they, who walk in the light of the proud world, know not!"

[98]
He now led me towards a rustic seat or alcove, beside which stood an image of that dark Deity, that God without a smile, who presides over the kingdom of the Dead.[4] The same livid and lifeless hue was upon his features, that hung over every thing in this dim valley; and, with his right hand, he pointed directly downwards, to denote that his melancholy kingdom lay there. A plantain—that favourite tree of the genii of Death—stood behind the statue, and spread its branches over the alcove, in which the Priest now, seating himself, signified that I should take my place by his side.

After a long pause, as if of thought and preparation,—"Nobly," said he, "young Greek, hast thou sustained the first trials of Initiation. What remains, though of vital import to the soul, brings with it neither pain nor peril to the body. Having now proved and chastened thy mortal frame, by the three ordeals of Fire,

---

[4] Osiris.

of Water, and of Air, the next task to which we are called is [99]
the purification of thy spirit,—the cleansing of that inward and
immortal part, so as to render it fit for the reception of the
last luminous revealment, when the Veils of the Sanctuary shall
be thrown aside, and the Great Secret of Secrets unfolded to
thee!—Towards this object, the primary and most essential step
is, instruction. What the three purifying elements, through which
thou hast passed, have done for thy body, instruction will effect
for——"

"But that lovely maiden!" I exclaimed, bursting from my
silence, having fallen, during his speech, into a deep revery,
in which I had forgotten him, myself, the Great Secret, every
thing—but her.

Startled by this profane interruption, he cast a look of alarm
towards the statue, as if fearful lest the God should have heard
my words. Then, turning to me, in a tone of mild solemnity, "It
is but too plain," said he, "that thoughts of the upper world, and [100]
of its vain delights, still engross thee too much, to let the lessons
of Truth sink profitably into thy heart. A few hours of meditation
amid this solemn scenery—of that wholesome meditation, which
purifies, by saddening—may haply dispose thee to receive, with
reverence, the holy and immortal knowledge that is in store for
thee. With this hope, I now leave thee to thy own thoughts, and
to that God, before whose calm and mournful eye the vanities of
the world, from which thou comest, wither!"

Thus saying, he turned slowly away, and passing behind the
statue, towards which he had pointed during the last sentence,
suddenly, and as if by enchantment, disappeared from my sight.

CHAP. IX.

Being left to my own solitary thoughts, I had now leisure to reflect, with coolness, on the inconveniences, if not dangers, of the situation into which my love of adventure had hurried me. However ready my imagination was to kindle, in its own ideal sphere, I have ever found that, when brought into contact with reality, it as suddenly cooled;—like those meteors, that seem stars in the air, but, the moment they touch earth, are extinguished. Such was the disenchantment that now succeeded to the dreams in which I had been indulging. As long as Fancy had the field of the future to herself, even immortality did not seem too distant a race for her. But when human instruments interposed, the illusion vanished. From mortal lips the promise of immortality seemed a mockery, and imagination herself had no wings that could carry beyond the grave.

Nor was this disappointment the only feeling that occupied me;—the imprudence of the step, which I had taken, now appeared in its full extent before my eyes. I had thrown myself into the power of the most artful priesthood in the world, without a chance of being able to escape from their toils, or to resist any machinations with which they might beset me. It seemed evident, from the state of preparation in which I had found all that wonderful apparatus, by which the terrors and splendours of Initiation are produced, that my descent into the pyramid was not unexpected. Numerous, indeed, and active as were the spies of the Sacred College of Memphis, there could be but little doubt that all my movements, since my arrival, had been tracked; and the many hours I had passed in watching and wandering round the pyramid, betrayed a curiosity which might well inspire these [103] wily priests with the hope of drawing an Epicurean into their superstitious toils.

I well knew their hatred to the sect of which I was Chief;—that they considered the Epicureans as, next to the Christians, the most formidable enemies of their craft and power. "How thought-less, then," I exclaimed, "to have placed myself in a situation, where I am equally helpless against their fraud and violence, and must either seem to be the dupe of their impostures, or submit to become the victim of their vengeance." Of these alternatives, bitter as they were, the latter appeared by far the more welcome. I blushed even to think of the mockeries to which I already had yielded; and the prospect of being put through still further ceremonials, and of being tutored and preached to by hypocrites I despised, appeared to me, in my present temper, a trial of patience, to which the flames and the whirlwinds I had already [104] encountered were pastime.

Often and impatiently did I look up, between those rocky walls, to the bright sky that appeared to rest upon their summits, as, round and round, through every part of the valley, I endeav-oured to find an outlet from its gloomy precincts. But in vain I endeavoured;—that rocky barrier, which seemed to end but in heaven, interposed itself every where. Neither did the image of the young maiden, though constantly in my mind, now bring with it the least consolation or hope. Of what avail was it that she, perhaps, was an inhabitant of this region, if I could neither see her smile, nor catch the sound of her voice,—if, while among preaching priests I wasted away my hours, her presence diffused its enchantment elsewhere.

At length exhausted, I lay down by the brink of the lake, and gave myself up to all the melancholy of my fancy. The pale [105] semblance of daylight, which had hitherto shone around, grew, every moment, more dim and dismal. Even the rich gleam, at the summit of the cascade, had faded; and the sunshine, like the water, exhausted in its descent, had now dwindled into a ghostly glimmer, far worse than darkness. The birds upon the lake, as if about to die with the dying light, sunk down their heads; and, as I looked to the statue, the deepening shadows gave an expression to its mournful features that chilled my very soul.

The thought of death, ever ready to present itself to my imagination, now came, with a disheartening weight, such as I had never before felt. I almost fancied myself already in the dark vestibule of the grave,—separated, for ever, from the world above, and with nothing but the blank of an eternal sleep before me. It had often, I knew, happened that the visitants of this mys-[106] terious realm were, after their descent from earth, never seen or heard of;—being condemned, for some failure in their initiatory trials, to pine away their lives in the dark dungeons, with which, as well as with altars, this region abounded. Such, I shuddered to think, might probably be my destiny; and so appalling was the thought, that even the spirit of defiance died within me, and I was already giving myself up to helplessness and despair.

At length, after some hours of this gloomy musing, I heard a rustling in the sacred grove behind the statue; and, soon after, the sound of the Priest's voice—more welcome than I had ever thought such voice could be—brought the assurance that I was not yet, at least, wholly abandoned. Finding his way to me through the gloom, he now led me to the same spot, on which we had parted so many hours before; and, in a voice that retained no trace of displeasure, bespoke my attention, while he should [107] reveal to me some of those divine truths, by whose infusion, he said, into the soul of man, its purification can alone be effected.

The valley had now become so wholly dark, that we could no longer discern each other's faces, as we sat. There was a melancholy in the voice of my instructor that well accorded with the gloom around us; and, saddened and subdued, I now listened with resignation, if not with interest, to those sublime, but, alas,

I thought, vain tenets, which, with the warmth of a believer, this Hierophant expounded to me.

He spoke of the pre-existence of the soul,—of its abode, from all eternity, in a place of bliss, of which all that we have most beautiful in our conceptions here is but a dim transcript, a clouded remembrance. In the blue depths of ether, he said, lay that "Country of the Soul,"—its boundary alone visible in the line of milky light, that separates it, as by a barrier of stars, from the dark earth. "Oh, realm of purity! Home of the yet [108] unfallen Spirit!—where, in the days of her primal innocence, she wandered, ere her beauty was soiled by the touch of earth, or her resplendent wings had withered away. Methinks," he cried, "I see, at this moment, those fields of radiance,—I look back, through the mists of life, into that luminous world, where the souls that have never lost their high, heavenly rank, still soar, without a stain, above the shadowless stars, and dwell together in infinite perfection and bliss!"

As he spoke these words, a burst of pure, brilliant light, like a sudden opening of heaven, broke through the valley; and, as soon as my eyes were able to endure the splendour, such a vision of loveliness and glory opened upon them, as took even my sceptical spirit by surprise, and made it yield, at once, to the potency of the spell.

Suspended, as I thought, in air, and occupying the whole of the opposite region of the valley, there appeared an immense orb [109] of light, within which, through a haze of radiance, I could see distinctly groups of young female spirits, who, in silent, but harmonious movement, like that of the stars, wound slowly through a variety of fanciful evolutions; and, as they linked and unlinked each other's arms, formed a living labyrinth of beauty and grace. Though their feet seemed to tread along a field of light, they had also wings, of the richest hue, which, like rainbows over waterfalls, when played with by the breeze, at every moment reflected a new variety of glory.

As I stood, gazing with wonder, the orb, with all its ethereal inmates, gradually receded into the dark void, lessening, as it went, and growing more bright, as it lessened;—till, at length, distant, apparently, as a retiring comet, this little world of Spirits, in one small point of intense radiance, shone its last and vanished. "Go," exclaimed the rapt Priest, "ye happy souls, of whose
[110] dwelling a glimpse is thus given to our eyes, go, wander, in your orb, through the boundless heaven, nor ever let a thought of this perishable world come to mingle its dross with your divine nature, or tempt you to that earthward fall, by which spirits, as bright, have been ruined!"

A pause ensued, during which, still under the influence of wonder, I sent my fancy wandering after the inhabitants of that orb,—almost wishing myself credulous enough to believe in a heaven, of which creatures, so like all that I most loved on earth, were inmates.

At length, the Priest, with a sigh at the contrast he was about to draw, between the happy spirits we had just seen and the fallen ones of earth, resumed his melancholy History of the Soul. Tracing it, from the first moment of earthward desire, to its final eclipse in the shadows of this world, he dwelt upon every stage of its darkening descent, with a pathos that sent sadness into the very depths of the heart. The first downward look of the
[111] Spirit towards earth—the tremble of her wings on the edge of Heaven—the giddy slide, at length, down that fatal descent, and the Lethæan cup, midway in the sky, of which when she has once tasted, Heaven is forgot,—through all these gradations he mournfully traced her fall, to the last stage of darkness, when, wholly immersed in this world, her celestial nature is changed, she can no longer rise above earth, nor remembers her home, but by glimpses so vague, that, mistaking for hope what is only memory, she believes them to be a light from the Future, not the Past.

"To retrieve this ruin of the once blessed Soul—to clear away, from around her, the clouds of earth, and, restoring her lost wings[5], facilitate their return to Heaven—such," said the reverend man, "is the great task of our religion, and such the triumph of those divine Mysteries, in which the life and essence of our [112] religion lie. However sunk and changed and clouded may be the Spirit, as long as a single trace of her original light remains, there is yet hope that——"

Here his voice was interrupted by a strain of mournful music, of which the low, distant breathings had been, for some minutes, heard, but which now gained upon the ear too thrillingly to let it listen to any more earthly sound. A faint light, too, at that instant broke through the valley,—and I could perceive, not far from the spot where we sat, a female figure, veiled, and crouching to earth, as if subdued by sorrow, or under the influence of shame.

The light, by which I saw her, was from a pale, moon-like meteor, which had formed itself in the air as the music approached, and shed over the rocks and the lake a glimmer as cold as that by which the Dead, in their own realm, gaze on each other. The music, too, which appeared to rise directly out of the lake, and to [113] come full of the breath of its dark waters, spoke a despondency in every note which no language could express;—and, as I listened to its tones, and looked upon that fallen Spirit, (for such, the holy man whispered, was the form before us,) so entirely did the illusion of the scene take possession of me, that, with breathless anxiety, I waited the result.

Nor had I gazed long before that form rose slowly from its drooping position;—the air around it grew bright, and the pale meteor overhead assumed a more cheerful and living light. The veil, which had before shrouded the face of the figure, became gradually transparent, and the features, one by one, disclosed themselves through it. Having tremblingly watched the progress of the apparition, I now started from my seat, and half exclaimed,

---

[5] In the language of Plato, Hierocles, &c. to "restore to the soul its wings," is the main object both of religion and philosophy.

[114]

"It is she!" In another minute, this veil had, like a thin mist, melted away, and the young Priestess of the Moon stood, for the third time, revealed before my eyes.

To rush instantly towards her was my first impulse—but the arm of the Priest held me firmly back. The fresh light, which had begun to flow in from all sides, collected itself in a glory round the spot where she stood. Instead of melancholy music, strains of the most exalted rapture were heard; and the young maiden, buoyant as the inhabitants of the fairy orb, amid a blaze of light like that which fell upon her in the Temple, ascended into the air.

"Stay, beautiful vision, stay!" I exclaimed, as, breaking from the hold of the Priest, I flung myself prostrate on the ground,—the only mode by which I could express the admiration, even to worship, with which I was filled. But the vanishing spirit heard me not:—receding into the darkness, like that orb, whose track she seemed to follow, her form lessened away, till she was seen no

[115]

more. Gazing, till the last luminous speck had disappeared, I suffered myself unconsciously to be led away by my reverend guide, who, placing me once more on my bed of poppy-leaves, left me to such repose as it was possible, after such a scene, to enjoy.

CHAP. X.

The apparition with which I had been blessed in that Valley of Visions—as the place where I had witnessed these wonders was called—brought back to my heart all the hopes and fancies, in which I had indulged during my descent from earth. I had now seen once more that matchless creature, who had been my guiding star into this mysterious world; and that she was, in some way, connected with the further revelations that awaited me, I saw no reason to doubt. There was a sublimity, too, in the doctrines of my reverend teacher, and even a hope in the promises of immortality held out by him, which, in spite of reason, won insensibly both upon my fancy and my pride.

The Future, however, was now but of secondary considera- tion;—the Present, and that deity of the Present, woman, were the objects that engrossed my whole soul. For the sake, indeed, of such beings alone did I think immortality desirable, nor, without them, would eternal life have appeared to me worth a prayer. To every further trial of my patience and faith, I now made up my mind to submit without a murmur. Some propitious chance, I fondly persuaded myself, might yet bring me nearer to the object of my adoration, and enable me to address, as mortal woman, her who had hitherto been to me but as a vision, a shade.

The period of my probation, however, was nearly at an end. Both frame and spirit had now been tried; and, as the crowning test of the purification of the latter was that power of seeing into the world of spirits, with which, in the Valley of Visions, I had proved myself to be endowed, there remained now, to perfect my Initiation, but this one night more, when, in the Temple of [118] Isis, and in the presence of her unveiled image, the last grand revelation of the Secret of Secrets was to open upon me.

I passed the morning of this day in company with the same venerable personage, who had, from the first, presided over the ceremonies of my instruction; and who, to inspire me with due reverence for the power and magnificence of his religion, now conducted me through the long range of illuminated galleries and shrines, that extend under the site upon which Memphis and the Pyramids stand, and form a counterpart under ground to that mighty city of temples upon earth.

He then descended with me, still lower, into those winding crypts, where lay the Seven Tables of stone, found by Hermes in the valley of Hebron. "On these tables," said he, "is written all the knowledge of the antediluvian race,—the decrees of the stars from the beginning of time, the annals of a still earlier world, [119] and all the marvellous secrets, both of heaven and earth, which would have been,

> "*but* for this key,
> Lost in the Universal Sea."

Returning to the region, from which we had descended, we next visited, in succession, a series of small shrines, representing the various objects of adoration through Egypt, and thus furnishing to the Priest an occasion for explaining the mysterious nature of animal worship, and the refined doctrines of theology that lay veiled under its forms. Every shrine was consecrated to a particular faith, and contained a living image of the deity which it adored. Beside the goat of Mendes, with his refulgent star upon his breast, I saw the crocodile, as presented to the eyes of its idolaters at Arsinoë, with costly gems in its loathsome ears, and rich bracelets of gold encircling its feet. Here, floating through a tank in the centre of a temple, the sacred carp of Lepidotum [120] exhibited its silvery scales; while, there, the Isiac serpents trailed languidly over the altar, with that movement which most inspires the hopes of their votaries. In one of the small chapels we found a beautiful child, feeding and watching over those golden beetles, which are adored for their brightness, as emblems of the sun; while, in another, stood a sacred ibis upon its pedestal, so like, in plumage and attitude, to the bird of the young Priestess, that I could gladly have knelt down and worshipped it for her sake.

After visiting these various shrines, and listening to the reflections which they suggested, I was next led by my guide to the Great Hall of the Zodiac, on whose ceiling, in bright and undying colours, was delineated the map of the firmament, as it appeared at the first dawn of time. Here, in pointing out the track of the sun, among the spheres, he spoke eloquently of the analogy that exists between moral and physical darkness—of the sympathy with which all spiritual creatures regard the sun, so as [121] to sadden and droop when he sinks into his wintry hemisphere, and to rejoice when he resumes his own empire of light. Hence, the festivals and hymns, with which most of the nations of the earth are wont to welcome the resurrection of his orb in spring, as an emblem and pledge of the re-ascent of the soul to heaven. Hence, the songs of sorrow, the mournful ceremonies,—like those Mysteries of the Night, upon the Lake of Saïs,—in which they brood over his autumnal descent into the shades, as a type of the Spirit's fall into this world of death.

In discourses such as these the hours passed away; and though there was nothing in the light of this sunless region to mark to the eye the decline of day, my own feelings told me that the night drew near;—nor, in spite of my incredulity, could I refrain from a flutter of hope, as that promised moment of revelation [122] approached, when the Mystery of Mysteries was to be made all my own. This consummation, however, was less near than I expected. My patience had still further trials to encounter. It was necessary, I now found, that I should keep watch, during the greater part of the night, in the Sanctuary of the Temple, alone and in darkness,—and thus prepare myself, by meditation, for the awful moment, when the irradiation from behind the sacred Veils was to burst upon me.

At the appointed hour, we left the Hall of the Zodiac, and proceeded through a line of long marble galleries, where the lamps were more thinly scattered as we advanced, till, at length, we found ourselves in total darkness. Here the Priest, taking me by the hand, and leading me down a flight of steps, into a place where the same deep gloom prevailed, said, with a voice trembling, as if from excess of awe,—"Thou art now in the Sanctuary of our goddess, Isis, and the dark veils, that hang over her image, are before thee!"

[123]

After exhorting me earnestly to that train of thought, which best accorded with the spirit of the place where I stood, and, above all, to that full and unhesitating faith, with which alone, he said, the manifestation of such mysteries should be approached, the holy man took leave of me, and re-ascended the steps;—while, so spell-bound did I feel by that deep darkness, that the last sound of his footsteps died upon my ear, before I ventured to stir a limb from the position in which he had left me.

The prospect of the long watch, now before me, was dreadful. Even danger itself, in an active form, would have been preferable to this sort of safe, but dull, probation, by which patience was the only virtue put to the proof. Having ascertained how far the space around me was free from obstacles, I endeavoured to beguile the time by pacing up and down within those limits, till I became tired of the echoes of my own tread. Finding my way, then, to what I felt to be a massive pillar, and, leaning wearily against it, I surrendered myself to a train of thoughts and feelings, far different from those with which the Hierophant had hoped to inspire me.

[124]

"Why," I again asked, "if these priests possess the secret of life, why are they themselves the victims of death? why sink into the grave with the cup of immortality in their hands? But no, safe boasters, the eternity they so lavishly promise is reserved for *another*, a future world—that ready resource of all priestly promises—that depository of the airy pledges of all creeds. Another world!—alas, where does it lie? or, what spirit hath ever come to say that Life is there?"

The conclusion, to which, half sadly, half passionately, I arrived, was that, life being but a dream of the moment, never [125] to come again, every bliss that is promised for hereafter should be secured by the wise man here. And, as no heaven I had ever heard of from these visionary priests opened half such certainty of happiness as that smile which I beheld last night,—"Let me," I exclaimed, impatiently, striking the massy pillar, till it rung, "let me but make that beautiful Priestess my own, and I here willingly exchange for her every chance of immortality, that the combined wisdom of Egypt's Twelve Temples can offer me!"

No sooner had I uttered these words, than a tremendous peal, like that of thunder, rolled over the Sanctuary, and seemed to shake its walls. On every side, too, a succession of blue, vivid flashes pierced, like so many lances of light, through the gloom, revealing to me, at intervals, the mighty dome in which I stood—its ceiling of azure, studded with stars, its colossal columns, towering aloft, and those dark, mysterious veils, which [126] hung, in massy drapery, from the roof to the floor, and covered the rich glories of the Shrine under their folds.

So weary had I grown of my tedious watch, that this stormy and fitful illumination, during which the Sanctuary seemed to rock to its base, was by no means an unwelcome interruption of the monotony under which my impatience suffered. After a short interval, however, the flashes ceased;—the sounds died away, like exhausted thunder, through the abyss, and darkness and silence, like that of the grave, succeeded.

Resting my back once more against the pillar, and fixing my eyes upon that side of the Sanctuary, from which the promised irradiation was to burst, I now resolved to await the awful moment in patience. Resigned and immovable, I had remained thus, for nearly another hour, when, suddenly, along the edges of the [127] mighty Veils, I perceived a thin rim of light, as if from some brilliant object under them;—like that border which encircles a cloud at sunset, when the radiance, from behind, is escaping at its edges.

This indication of concealed glories grew every instant more strong; till, at last, vividly marked as it was upon the darkness, the narrow fringe of lustre almost pained the eye, giving promise of a splendour too bright to be endured. My expectations were now wound to the highest pitch, and all the scepticism, into which I had been cooling down my mind, was forgotten. The wonders that had been presented to me since my descent from earth—that glimpse into Elysium on the first night of my coming—those visitants from the Land of Spirits in the mysterious valley,—all led me to expect, in this last and brightest revelation, such visions of glory and knowledge as might transcend even fancy itself, nor [128] leave a doubt that they belonged less to earth than heaven.

While, with an imagination thus excited, I stood waiting the result, an increased gush of light still more awakened my attention; and I saw, with an intenseness of interest, which made my heart beat aloud, one of the corners of the mighty Veil slowly raised up. I now felt that the Great Secret—whatever it might be—was at hand. A vague hope even crossed my mind—so wholly had imagination resumed her empire—that the splendid promise of my dream was on the point of being realised!

With surprise, however, and—for a moment—with disappointment, I perceived, that the massy corner of the Veil was but raised sufficiently to allow a female figure to emerge from under it,—and then fell again, over its mystic splendours, as dark as before. By the strong light, too, that issued when the drapery [129] was lifted, and illuminated the profile of the emerging figure, I either saw, or fancied that I saw, the same bright features, that had already mocked me so often with their momentary charm, and seemed destined to haunt my heart as unavailingly as the fond, vain dream of Immortality itself.

Dazzled as I had been by that short gush of splendour, and distrusting even my senses, when under the influence of a fancy so excited, I had hardly time to question myself as to the reality of my impression, when I heard the sounds of light footsteps approaching me through the gloom. In a second or two more, the figure stopped before me, and, placing the end of a riband gently in my hand, said, in a tremulous whisper, "Follow, and be silent."

So sudden and strange was the adventure, that, for a moment, I hesitated,—fearful lest my eyes should have been deceived as to the object they had seen. Casting a look towards the Veil, which seemed bursting with its luminous secret, I was almost doubting [130] to which of the two chances I should commit myself, when I felt the riband in my hand pulled softly at the other extremity. This movement, at once, like a touch of magic, decided me. Without further deliberation, I yielded to the silent summons, and following my guide, who was already at some distance before me, found myself led up the same flight of marble steps, by which the Priest had conducted me into the Sanctuary. Arrived at their summit, I felt the pace of my conductress quicken, and, giving one more look to the Veiled Shrine, whose glories we left burning ineffectually behind us, hastened into the gloom, full of confidence in the belief, that she, who now held the other end of that clue, was one whom I could follow devotedly through the world.

CHAP. XI.

So rapidly was I hurried along by my unseen conductress, full of wonder at the speed with which she ventured through these labyrinths, that I had but little time to reflect upon the strangeness of the adventure to which I had committed myself. My knowledge of the character of the priests, as well as the fearful rumours that had reached me, of the fate that often attended unbelievers in their hands, waked a momentary suspicion of treachery in my mind. But, when I recalled the face of my guide, as I had seen it in the chapel, with that divine look, the very memory of which brought purity into the heart, this suspicion all vanished, and I felt shame at having harboured it but an instant.

In the mean while, our course continued uninterrupted, through windings more capriciously intricate than any that I had yet passed, and whose darkness seemed never to have been disturbed by a single glimmer. My conductress still continued at some distance before me, and the clue, to which I clung as if it were the thread of Destiny herself, was still kept, by her speed, at full stretch between us. At length, suddenly stopping, she said, in a breathless whisper, "Seat thyself here," and, at the same moment, led me by the hand to a sort of low car, in which I lost not a moment in placing myself, as desired, while the maiden, as promptly, took her seat by my side.

A sudden click, like the touching of a spring, was then heard, and the car,—which, as I had felt in entering it, leaned half-way over a steep descent,—on being loosed from its station, shot down, almost perpendicularly, into the darkness, with a rapidity

which, at first, nearly deprived me of breath. The wheels slid
smoothly and noiselessly in grooves, and the impetus, which the   [133]
car acquired in descending, was sufficient, I perceived, to carry
it up an eminence that succeeded,—from the summit of which
it again rushed down another declivity, even still more long and
precipitous than the former. In this manner we proceeded, by
alternate falls and rises, till, at length, from the last and steepest
elevation, the car descended upon a level of deep sand, where,
after running for a few yards, it by degrees lost its motion and
stopped.

Here, the maiden alighting, again placed the riband in my
hands,—and again I followed her, though with more slowness
and difficulty than before, as our way led up a flight of damp and
time-worn steps, whose ascent seemed to the weary and insecure
foot interminable. Perceiving with what languor my guide now
advanced, I was on the point of making an effort to assist her
progress, when the creak of an opening door above, and a faint
gleam of light which, at the same moment, shone upon her figure,   [134]
apprised me that we were arrived within reach of sunshine.

Joyfully I followed through this opening, and, by the dim light,
could discern, that we were now in the sanctuary of a vast, ruined
temple,—having entered by a passage under the lofty pedestal,
upon which an image of the idol of the place once stood. The
first movement of the maiden, after replacing the portal under
the pedestal, was, without even a look towards me, to cast herself
down on her knees, with her hands clasped and uplifted, as if
for the purpose of thanksgiving or prayer. But she was unable to
sustain herself in this position;—her strength could hold out no
longer. Overcome by agitation and fatigue, she sunk senseless
upon the pavement.

Bewildered as I was, myself, by the events of the night, I stood
for some minutes looking upon her in a state of helplessness and
alarm. But, reminded, by my own feverish sensations, of the   [135]
reviving effects of the air, I raised her gently in my arms, and

crossing the corridor that surrounded the sanctuary, found my way to the outer vestibule of the temple. Here, shading her eyes from the sun, I placed her, reclining, upon the steps, where the cool wind, then blowing freshly from the north, might play, with free draught, between the pillars over her brow.

It was, indeed,—I now saw, with certainty,—the same beautiful and mysterious girl, who had been the cause of my descent into that subterranean world, and who now, under such strange and unaccountable circumstances, was my guide back again to the realms of day. I looked round, to discover where we were, and beheld such a scene of grandeur, as—could my eyes have wandered to any other object from the pale form reclining at my side—might well have won them to dwell on its splendid beauties.

[136] I was now standing, I found, on the small island in the centre of Lake Mœris; and that sanctuary, where we had emerged from darkness, formed part of the ruins of a temple, which (as I have since learned) was, in the grander days of Memphis, a place of pilgrimage for worshippers from all parts of Egypt. The fair Lake, itself, out of whose waters once rose pavilions, palaces, and even lofty pyramids, was still, though divested of many of these wonders, a scene of interest and splendour such as the whole world could not equal. While the shores still sparkled with mansions and temples, that bore testimony to the luxury of a living race, the voice of the Past, speaking out of unnumbered ruins, whose summits, here and there, rose blackly above the wave, told of times long fled and generations long swept away, before whose giant remains all the glory of the present stood humbled. Over the southern bank of the Lake hung the dark relics of the Labyrinth;—its twelve Royal Palaces, like the mansions of the [137] Zodiac,—its thundering portals and constellated halls, having left nothing behind but a few frowning ruins, which, contrasted with the soft groves of olive and acacia around them, seemed to rebuke the luxuriant smiles of nature, and threw a melancholy

grandeur over the whole scene.

The effects of the air, in re-animating the young Priestess, were less speedy than I had expected;—her eyes were still closed, and she remained pale and insensible. Alarmed, I now rested her head (which had been, for some time, supported by my arm,) against the base of a column, with my cloak for its pillow, while I hastened to procure some water from the Lake. The temple stood high, and the descent to the shore was precipitous. But, my Epicurean habits having but little impaired my activity, I soon descended, with the lightness of a desert deer, to the bottom. Here, plucking from a lofty bean-tree, whose flowers stood, shining like gold, above the water, one of those large hollowed [138] leaves that serve as cups for the Hebes of the Nile, I filled it from the Lake, and hurried back with the cool draught to the temple. It was not without some difficulty and delay that I succeeded, in bearing my rustic chalice steadily up the steep; more than once did an unlucky slip waste its contents, and as often did I impatiently return to refill it.

During this time, the young maiden was fast recovering her animation and consciousness; and, at the moment when I appeared above the edge of the steep, was just rising from the steps, with her hand pressed to her forehead, as if confusedly recalling the recollection of what had occurred. No sooner did she observe me, than a short cry of alarm broke from her lips. Looking anxiously round, as though she sought for protection, and half audibly uttering the words, "Where is he?" she made an effort, as I approached, to retreat into the temple. [139]

Already, however, I was by her side, and taking her hand gently, as she turned away, "Whom dost thou seek, fair Priestess?" I asked,—for the first time breaking through the silence she had enjoined, and in a tone that might have re-assured the most timid spirit. But my words had no effect in calming her apprehension. Trembling, and with her eyes still averted towards the Temple, she continued in a voice of suppressed alarm,—"Where *can* he be?—that venerable Athenian, that philosopher, who——"

"Here, here," I exclaimed, anxiously interrupting her,—"behold him still by thy side—the same, the very same who saw thee steal from under the lighted Veils of the Sanctuary, whom thou hast guided by a clue through those labyrinths below, and who now but waits his command from those lips, to devote himself through life and death to thy service." As I spoke these words, she turned slowly round, and looking timidly in my face, while her own burned with blushes, said, in a tone of doubt and wonder, "Thou!" and hid her eyes in her hands.

[140]

I knew not how to interpret a reception so unexpected. That some mistake or disappointment had occurred was evident; but so inexplicable did the whole adventure appear, that it was in vain to think of unravelling any part of it. Weak and agitated, she now tottered to the steps of the temple, and there seating herself, with her forehead against the cold marble, seemed for some moments absorbed in the most anxious thought,—while silent and watchful I waited her decision, with a prophetic feeling, however, that my destiny would be henceforth linked with hers.

The inward struggle by which she was agitated, though violent, was not of long continuance. Starting suddenly from her seat, with a look of terror towards the temple, as if the fear of immediate pursuit had alone decided her, she pointed eagerly towards the East, and exclaimed, "To the Nile, without delay!"—clasping her hands, when she had spoken, with the most suppliant fervour, as if to soften the abruptness of the mandate she had given, and appealing to me with a look that would have taught Stoics tenderness.

[141]

I lost no time in obeying the welcome command. While a thousand wild hopes and wishes crowded upon my fancy, at the prospect which a voyage, under such auspices, presented, I descended rapidly to the shore, and hailing one of the numerous boats that ply upon the Lake for hire, arranged speedily for a passage down the canal to the Nile. Having learned, too, from the boatmen, a more easy path up the rock, I hastened back to the Temple for my fair charge; and without a word, a look, that could alarm, even by its kindness, or disturb that innocent confidence which she now placed in me, led her down by the winding path [142] to the boat.

Every thing looked smiling around us as we embarked. The morning was now in its first freshness, and the path of the breeze might be traced over the Lake, wakening up its waters from their sleep of the night. The gay, golden-winged birds that haunt these shores, were, in every direction, skimming along the lake; while, with a graver consciousness of beauty, the swan and the pelican were seen dressing their white plumage in the mirror of its wave. To add to the animation of the scene, a sweet tinkling of musical instruments came, at intervals, on the breeze, from boats at a distance, employed thus early in pursuing the fish of these waters, that suffer themselves to be decoyed into the nets by music.

The vessel which I selected for our voyage was one of those small pleasure-boats or yachts,—so much in use among the lux-urious navigators of the Nile,—in the centre of which rises a [143] pavilion of cedar or cypress wood, gilded gorgeously, without, with religious emblems, and fitted up, within, for all the purposes of feasting and repose. To the door of this pavilion I now led my companion, and, after a few words of kindness—tempered with as much respectful reserve as the deep tenderness which I felt would admit of—left her in solitude to court that restoring rest, which the agitation of her spirits but too much required.

For myself, though repose was hardly less necessary to me, the ferment in which my thoughts had been kept seemed to render it hopeless. Throwing myself upon the deck, under an awning which the sailors had raised for me, I continued, for some hours, in a sort of vague day-dream,—sometimes passing in review the scenes of that subterranean drama, and sometimes, with my eyes fixed in drowsy vacancy, receiving passively the impressions of [144] the bright scenery through which we passed.

The banks of the canal were then luxuriantly wooded. Under the tufts of the light and towering palm were seen the orange and the citron, interlacing their boughs; while, here and there, huge tamarisks thickened the shade, and, at the very edge of the bank, the willow of Babylon stood bending its graceful branches into the water. Occasionally, out of the depth of these groves, there shone a small temple or pleasure-house;—while, now and then, an opening in their line of foliage allowed the eye to wander over extensive fields, all covered with beds of those pale, sweet roses, for which this district of Egypt is so celebrated.

The activity of the morning hour was visible every where. Flights of doves and lapwings were fluttering among the leaves, and the white heron, which had roosted all night in some date-tree, now stood sunning its wings upon the green bank, or floated, like living silver, over the flood. The flowers, too, both of land and water, looked freshly awakened;—and, most of all, the superb lotus, which had risen with the sun from the wave, and was now holding up her chalice for a full draught of his light.

Such were the scenes that now passed before my eyes, and mingled with the reveries that floated through my mind, as our boat, with its high, capacious sail, swept over the flood. Though the occurrences of the last few days appeared to me one series of wonders, yet by far the most miraculous wonder of all was, that she, whose first look had sent wild-fire into my heart,—whom I had thought of ever since with a restlessness of passion, that would have dared any thing on earth to obtain its object,—was now sleeping sacredly in that small pavilion, while guarding her, even from myself, I lay calmly at its threshold.

Meanwhile, the sun had reached his meridian. The busy hum of the morning had died gradually away, and all around was sleeping in the hot stillness of noon. The Nile-goose, folding her splendid wings, was lying motionless on the shadow of the sycamores in the water. Even the nimble lizards upon the bank seemed to move more languidly, as the light fell upon their gold and azure hues. Overcome as I was with watching, and weary with thought, it was not long before I yielded to the becalming influence of the hour. Looking fixedly at the pavilion,—as if once more to assure my senses, that I was not already in a dream, but that the young Egyptian was really there,—I felt my eyes close as I looked, and in a few minutes sunk into a profound sleep.

CHAP. XII.

It was by the canal through which we now sailed, that, in the more prosperous days of Memphis, the commerce of Upper Egypt and Nubia was transported to her magnificent Lake, and from thence, having paid tribute to the queen of cities, was poured out again, through the Nile, into the ocean. The course of this canal to the river was not direct, but ascending in a south-easterly direction towards the Saïd; and in calms, or with adverse winds, the passage was tedious. But as the breeze was now blowing freshly from the north, there was every prospect of our reaching the river before night-fall. Rapidly, too, as our galley swept along the flood, its motion was so smooth as to be hardly felt; and the quiet gurgle of the waters underneath, and the drowsy song of the boatman at the prow, alone disturbed the deep silence that prevailed.

The sun, indeed, had nearly sunk behind the Libyan hills, before the sleep, in which these sounds lulled me, was broken; and the first object, on which my eyes rested, in waking, was that fair young Priestess,—seated under a porch by which the door of the pavilion was shaded, and bending intently over a small volume that lay unrolled on her lap.

Her face was but half turned towards me, and as, once or twice, she raised her eyes to the warm sky, whose light fell, softened through the trellis, over her cheek, I found every feeling of reverence, with which she had inspired me in the chapel, return. There was even a purer and holier charm around her countenance, thus seen by the natural light of day, than in those dim and unhallowed regions below. She could now, too, look direct to the glorious sky, and that heaven and her eyes, so worthy of each other, met.   [149]

After contemplating her for a few moments, with little less than adoration, I rose gently from my resting-place, and approached the pavilion. But the mere movement had startled her from her devotion, and, blushing and confused, she covered the volume with the folds of her robe.

In the art of winning upon female confidence, I had long been schooled; and, now that to the lessons of gallantry the inspiration of love was added, my ambition to please and to interest could hardly, it may be supposed, fail of success. I soon found, however, how much less fluent is the heart than the fancy, and how very distinct are the operations of making love and feeling it. In the few words of greeting now exchanged between us, it was evident that the gay, the enterprising Epicurean was little less embarrassed than the secluded Priestess;—and, after one or two ineffectual efforts to bring our voices acquainted with each [150] other, the eyes of both turned bashfully away, and we relapsed into silence.

From this situation—the result of timidity on one side, and of a feeling altogether new, on the other—we were, at length, after an interval of estrangement, relieved, by the boatmen announcing that the Nile was in sight. The countenance of the young Egyptian brightened at this intelligence; and the smile with which I congratulated her on the speed of our voyage was answered by another, so full of gratitude, that already an instinctive sympathy seemed established between us.

We were now on the point of entering that sacred river, of whose sweet waters the exile drinks in his dreams,—for a draught of whose flood the daughters of the Ptolemies, when wedded to foreign kings, sighed in the midst of their splendour. As our boat, with slackened sail, glided into the current, an enquiry [151] from the boatmen, whether they should anchor for the night in the Nile, first reminded me of the ignorance, in which I still remained, with respect to either the motive or destination of our voyage. Embarrassed by their question I directed my eyes towards the Priestess, whom I saw waiting for my answer with a look of anxiety, which this silent reference to her wishes at once dispelled. Eagerly unfolding the volume with which I had seen her occupied, she took from its folds a small leaf of papyrus, on which there appeared to be some faint lines of drawing, and after thoughtfully looking upon it, herself, for a moment, placed it, with an agitated hand, in mine.

In the mean time, the boatmen had taken in their sail, and the yacht drove slowly down the river with the current, while, by a light which had been kindled at sunset on the deck, I stood [152] examining the leaf that the Priestess had given me,—her dark eyes fixed anxiously on my countenance all the while. The lines traced upon the papyrus were so faint as to be almost invisible, and I was for some time at a loss to divine their import. At length, I could perceive that they were the outlines, or map—traced slightly and unsteadily with a Memphian reed—of a part of that mountainous ridge by which Upper Egypt is bounded to the east, together with the names, or rather emblems, of the chief towns in the neighbourhood.

It was thither, I could not doubt, that the young Priestess wished to pursue her course. Without a moment's delay, there-fore, I gave orders to the boatmen to set our yacht before the wind and ascend the current. My command was promptly obeyed: the white sail again rose into the region of the breeze, and the satis-faction that beamed in every feature of the fair Egyptian showed that the quickness with which I had obeyed her wishes was not [153] unfelt by her. The moon had now risen; and though the current was against us, the Etesian wind of the season blew strongly up the river, and we were soon floating before it, through the rich plains and groves of the Saïd.

The love, with which this simple girl had inspired me,

was—possibly from the mystic scenes and situations in which I had seen her—not unmingled with a tinge of superstitious awe, under the influence of which I felt the buoyancy of my spirit checked. The few words that had passed between us on the subject of our route had somewhat loosened this spell; and what I wanted of vivacity and confidence was more than made up by the tone of deep sensibility which love had awakened in their place.

We had not proceeded far before the glittering of lights at a distance, and the shooting up of fireworks, at intervals, into the air, apprised us that we were approaching one of those night-fairs, or marts, which it is the custom, at this season, to hold upon the [154] Nile. To me the scene was familiar; but to my young companion it was evidently a new world; and the mixture of alarm and delight with which she gazed, from under her veil, upon the busy scene into which we now sailed, gave an air of innocence to her beauty, which still more heightened its every charm.

It was one of the widest parts of the river; and the whole surface, from one bank to the other, was covered with boats. Along the banks of a green island, in the middle of the stream, lay anchored the galleys of the principal traders,—large floating bazaars, bearing each the name of its owner, emblazoned in letters of flame, upon the stern. Over their decks were spread out, in gay confusion, the products of the loom and needle of Egypt,—rich carpets of Memphis, and those variegated veils, for which the female embroiderers of the Nile are so celebrated, and to which the name of Cleopatra lends a traditional value. In each of the other galleys was exhibited some branch of Egyptian [155] workmanship,—vases of the fragrant porcelain of On,—cups of that frail crystal, whose hues change like those of the pigeon's plumage,—enamelled amulets graven with the head of Anubis, and necklaces and bracelets of the black beans of Abyssinia.

While Commerce thus displayed her luxuries in one quarter, in every other direction Pleasure, multiplied into her thousand

shapes, swarmed over the waters. Nor was the festivity confined
to the river only. All along the banks of the island and on the
shores, lighted up mansions were seen through the trees, from
which sounds of music and merriment came. In some of the
boats were bands of minstrels, who, from time to time, answered
each other, like echoes, across the wave; and the notes of the
lyre, the flageolet, and the sweet lotus-wood flute, were heard,
in the pauses of revelry, dying along the waters.

[156]   Meanwhile, from other boats stationed in the least lighted
places, the workers of fire sent forth their wonders into the air.
Bursting out from time to time, as if in the very exuberance of
joy, these sallies of flame seemed to reach the sky, and there
breaking into a shower of sparkles, shed such a splendour round,
as brightened even the white Arabian hills,—making them shine
like the brow of Mount Atlas at night, when the fire from his
own bosom is playing around its snows.

The opportunity which this luxurious mart afforded us, of
providing ourselves with other and less remarkable habiliments
than those in which we had escaped from that nether world,
was too seasonable not to be gladly taken advantage of by both.
For myself, the strange mystic garb that I wore was sufficiently
concealed by my Grecian mantle, which I had luckily thrown
round me on the night of my watch. But the thin veil of my
companion was a far less efficient disguise. She had, indeed,
[157]   flung away the golden beetles from her hair; but the sacred robe
of her order was still too visible, and the stars of the bandelet
shone brightly through her veil.

Most gladly, therefore, did she avail herself of this opportunity
of a change; and, as she took from a casket—which, with the
volume I had seen her reading, appeared to be her only treasure—a small jewel, to exchange for the simple garments she
had chosen, there fell out, at the same time, the very cross of
silver, which I had seen her kiss, as may be remembered, in the
monumental chapel, and which was afterwards pressed to my

own lips. This link (for such it appeared to my imagination) between us, now revived in my heart all the burning feelings of that moment;—and, had I not abruptly turned away, my agitation would, but too plainly, have betrayed itself.

The object, for which we had delayed in this gay scene, being accomplished, the sail was again spread, and we proceeded on [158] our course up the river. The sounds and the lights we left behind died gradually away, and we now floated along in moonlight and silence once more. Sweet dews, worthy of being called "the tears of Isis," fell through the air, and every plant and flower sent its fragrance to meet them. The wind, just strong enough to bear us smoothly against the current, scarcely stirred the shadow of the tamarisks on the water. As the inhabitants from all quarters were collected at the night-fair, the Nile was more than usually still and solitary. Such a silence, indeed, prevailed, that, as we glided near the shore, we could hear the rustling of the acacias, as the chameleons ran up their stems. It was, altogether, a night such as only the clime of Egypt can boast, when every thing lies lulled in that sort of bright tranquillity, which, we may imagine, shines over the sleep of those happy spirits, who are supposed to rest in the Valley of the Moon, on their way to heaven. [159]

By such a light, and at such an hour, seated, side by side, on the deck of that bark, did we pursue our course up the lonely Nile—each a mystery to the other—our thoughts, our objects, our very names a secret;—separated, too, till now, by destinies so different, the one, a gay voluptuary of the Garden of Athens, the other, a secluded Priestess of the Temples of Memphis;—and the only relation yet established between us being that dangerous one of love, passionate love, on one side, and the most feminine and confiding dependence on the other.

The passing adventure of the night-fair had not only dispelled still more our mutual reserve, but had supplied us with a subject on which we could converse without embarrassment. From this topic I took care to lead on, without interruption, to others,—fear-

[160]

ful lest our former silence should return, and the music of her voice again be lost to me. It was, indeed, only by thus indirectly unburdening my heart that I was enabled to refrain from the full utterance of all I thought and felt; and the restless rapidity with which I flew from subject to subject was but an effort to escape from the only one in which my heart was interested.

"How bright and happy," said I,—pointing up to Sothis, the fair Star of the Waters, which was just then sparkling brilliantly over our heads,—"How bright and happy this world ought to be, if—as your Egyptian sages assert—yon pure and beautiful luminary was its birth-star!" Then, still leaning back, and letting my eyes wander over the firmament, as if seeking to disengage them from the fascination which they dreaded—"To the study (I said), for ages, of skies like this, may the pensive and mystic character of your nation be traced. That mixture of pride and melancholy which naturally arises, at the sight of those eternal lights shining

[161]

out of darkness;—that sublime, but saddened, anticipation of a Future, which comes over the soul in the silence of such an hour, when, though Death seems to reign in the repose of earth, there are those beacons of Immortality burning in the sky—"

Pausing, as I uttered the word "immortality," with a sigh to think how little my heart echoed to my lips, I looked in the face of the maiden, and saw that it had lighted up, as I spoke, into a glow of holy animation, such as Faith alone gives—such as Hope herself wears, when she is dreaming of heaven. Touched by the contrast, and gazing upon her with mournful tenderness, I found my arms half opened, to clasp her to my heart, while the words died away inaudibly upon my lips,—"thou, too, beautiful maiden! must thou, too, die for ever?"

My self-command, I felt, had nearly deserted me. Rising abruptly from my seat, I walked to the middle of the deck, and

[162]

stood, for some moments, unconsciously gazing upon one of those fires, which,—as is the custom of all who travel by night upon the Nile,—our boatmen had just kindled, to scare away the crocodiles from the vessel. But it was in vain that I endeavoured to compose my spirit. Every effort I made but more deeply convinced me, that, till the mystery which hung round that maiden should be solved—till the secret, with which my own bosom laboured, should be disclosed—it was fruitless to attempt even a semblance of tranquillity.

My resolution was therefore taken;—to lay open, at least, my own heart, as far as such a revelation might be risked, without startling the timid innocence of my companion. Thus resolved, I returned, with more composure, to my seat by her side, and taking from my bosom the small mirror which she had dropped in the Temple, and which I had ever since worn suspended round my neck, with a trembling hand presented it to her view. The boatmen had just kindled one of their night-fires near us, and its [163] light, as she leaned forward towards the mirror, fell on her face.

The quick blush of surprise with which she recognised it to be hers, and her look of bashful, yet eager, inquiry, in raising her eyes to mine, were appeals to which I was not, of course, slow in answering. Beginning with the first moment when I saw her in the Temple, and passing hastily, but with words that burned as they went, over the impression which she had then left upon my heart and fancy, I proceeded to describe the particulars of my descent into the pyramid—my surprise and adoration at the door of the chapel—my encounter with the Trials of Initiation, so mysteriously prepared for me, and all the various visionary wonders I had witnessed in that region, till the moment when I had seen her stealing from under the Veils to approach me.

Though, in detailing these events, I had said but little of the feelings they had awakened in me,—though my lips had sent [164] back many a sentence, unuttered, there was still enough that could neither be subdued or disguised, and which, like that light from under the veils of her own Isis, glowed through every word that I spoke. When I told of the scene in the chapel,—of the silent interview which I had witnessed between the dead and the living,—the maiden leaned down her head and wept, as from a heart full of tears. It seemed a pleasure to her, however, to listen; and, when she looked at me again, there was an earnest and affectionate cordiality in her eyes, as if the knowledge of my having been present at that mournful scene had opened a new source of sympathy and intelligence between us. So neighbouring are the fountains of Love and of Sorrow, and so imperceptibly do they often mingle their streams.

[165] Little, indeed, as I was guided by art or design, in my manner and conduct to this innocent girl, not all the most experienced gallantry of the Garden could have dictated a policy half so seductive as that which my new master, Love, now taught me. The ardour which, shown at once, and without reserve, might have startled a heart so little prepared for it, thus checked and softened by the timidity of real love, won its way without alarm, and, when most diffident of success, most triumphed. Like one whose sleep is gradually broken by music, the maiden's heart was awakened without being disturbed. She followed the charm, unconscious whither it led, nor was aware of the flame she had lighted in another's bosom, till she perceived the reflection of it glimmering in her own.

[166] Impatient as I was to appeal to her generosity and sympathy, for a similar proof of confidence to that which I had just given, the night was now too far advanced for me to impose such a task upon her. After exchanging a few words, in which, though little was said, there was a tone and manner that spoke far more than language, we took a lingering leave of each other for the night, with every prospect of still being together in our dreams.

CHAP. XIII.

It was so near the dawn of day when we parted, that we again found the sun sinking westward when we rejoined each other. The smile with which she met me,—so frankly cordial,—might have been taken for the greeting of a long mellowed friendship, did not the blush and the castdown eyelid, that followed, give symptoms of a feeling newer and less calm. For myself, lightened as I was, in some degree, by the confession which I had made, I was yet too conscious of the new aspect thus given to our intercourse, to feel altogether unembarrassed at the prospect of returning to the theme. It was, therefore, willingly we both suffered our attention to be diverted, by the variety of objects that presented themselves on the way, from a subject that both equally trembled to approach.

The river was now full of life and motion. Every moment we met with boats descending the current, so independent of aid from sail or oar, that the sailors sat idly upon the deck as they shot along, singing or playing upon their double-reeded pipes. Of these boats, the greater number came loaded with merchandise from Coptos,—some with those large emeralds, from the mine in the desert, whose colours, it is said, are brightest at the full of the moon, and some laden with frankincense from the acacia-groves near the Red Sea. On the decks of others, that had been to the Golden Mountains beyond Syene, were heaped blocks and fragments of that sweet-smelling wood, which the Green Nile of Nubia washes down in the season of the floods.

Our companions up the stream were far less numerous. Occasionally a boat, returning lightened from the fair of last night,

[169] with those high sails that catch every breeze from over the hills, shot past us;—while, now and then, we overtook one of those barges full of bees, that at this season of the year, are sent to colonise the gardens of the south, and take advantage of the first flowers after the inundation has passed away.

By these various objects we were, for a short time, enabled to divert the conversation from lighting and settling upon the one subject, round which it continually hovered. But the effort, as might be expected, was not long successful. As evening advanced, the whole scene became more solitary. We less frequently ventured to look upon each other, and our intervals of silence grew more long.

It was near sunset, when, in passing a small temple on the shore, whose porticoes were now full of the evening light, we saw, issuing from a thicket of acanthus near it, a train of young maids linked together in the dance by lotus-stems, held at arms'

[170] length between them. Their tresses were also wreathed with this emblem of the season, and such a profusion of the white flowers were twisted round their waists and arms, that they might have been taken, as they gracefully bounded along the bank, for Nymphs of the Nile, risen freshly from their gardens under the wave.

After looking for a few moments at this sacred dance, the maid turned away her eyes, with a look of pain, as if the remembrances it recalled were of no welcome nature. This momentary retrospect, this glimpse into the past, seemed to offer a sort of clue to the secret for which I panted;—and, gradually and delicately as my impatience would allow, I availed myself of it. Her frankness, however, saved me the embarrassment of much questioning. She even seemed to feel that the confidence I sought was due to me, and beyond the natural hesitation of maidenly modesty, not a shade of reserve or evasion appeared.

[171] To attempt to repeat, in her own touching words, the simple story which she now related to me, would be like endeavouring

to note down some strain of unpremeditated music, with those fugitive graces, those felicities of the moment, which no art can restore, as they first met the ear. From a feeling, too, of humility, she had omitted in her narrative some particulars relating to herself, which I afterwards learned;—while others, not less important, she but slightly passed over, from a fear of wounding the prejudices of her heathen hearer.

I shall, therefore, give her story, as the outline which she, herself, sketched was afterwards filled up by a pious and venerable hand,—far, far more worthy than mine of being associated with the memory of such purity.

STORY OF ALĒTHE.

"The mother of this maiden was the beautiful Theora of Alexandria, who, though a native of that city, was descended from Grecian parents. When very young, Theora was one of the seven maidens selected, to note down the discourses of the eloquent Origen, who, at that period, presided over the School of Alexandria, and was in all the fulness of his fame, both among Pagans and Christians. Endowed richly with the learning of both creeds, he brought the natural light of philosophy to elucidate the mysteries of faith, and was only proud of his knowledge of the wisdom of this world, inasmuch as it ministered to the triumph of divine truth.

"Though he had courted in vain the crown of martyrdom, it was held, throughout his life, suspended over his head, and in more than one persecution, he had evinced his readiness to die for that faith which he lived but to testify and adorn. On one of these occasions, his tormentors, having habited him like an Egyptian priest, placed him upon the steps of the Temple of Serapis, and commanded that he should, in the manner of the Pagan ministers, present palm-branches to the multitude who went up to the shrine. But the courageous Christian disappointed their views. Holding forth the branches with an unshrinking hand, he cried aloud, 'Come hither and take the branch, not of an Idol Temple, but of Christ.'

"So indefatigable was this learned Father in his studies, that, while composing his Commentary on the Scriptures, he was attended by seven scribes or notaries, who relieved each other in taking down the dictates of his eloquent tongue; while the same number of young females, selected for the beauty of their penmanship, were employed in arranging and transcribing the precious leaves.

"Among the scribes so selected, was the fair young Theora, [174] whose parents, though attached to the Pagan worship, were not unwilling to profit by the accomplishments of their daughter, thus devoted to a task which they considered purely mechanical. To the maid herself, however, her task brought far other feelings and consequences. She read anxiously as she wrote, and the divine truths, so eloquently illustrated, found their way, by degrees, from the page to her heart. Deeply, too, as the written words affected her, the discourses from the lips of the great teacher himself, which she had frequent opportunities of hearing, sunk still more deeply into her mind. There was, at once, a sublimity and gentleness in his views of religion, which, to the tender hearts and lively imaginations of women, never failed to appeal with convincing power. Accordingly, the list of his female pupils was numerous; and the names of Barbara, Juliana, Heraïs, and others, bear honourable testimony to his influence over that sex. [175]

"To Theora the feeling, with which his discourses inspired her, was like a new soul,—a consciousness of spiritual existence, unfelt before. By the eloquence of the comment she was awakened into admiration of the text; and when, by the kindness of a Catechumen of the school, who had been struck by her innocent zeal, she, for the first time, became possessor of a copy of the Scriptures, she could not sleep for thinking of her sacred treasure. With a mixture of pleasure and fear she hid it from all eyes, and was like one who had received a divine guest under her roof, and felt fearful of betraying its divinity to the world.

"A heart so awake would have been easily secured to the faith, had her opportunities of hearing the sacred word continued. But circumstances arose to deprive her of this advantage. The mild Origen, long harassed and thwarted in his labours by

[176] the tyranny of the Bishop of Alexandria, Demetrius, was obliged to relinquish his school and fly from Egypt. The occupation of the fair scribe was, therefore, at an end: her intercourse with the followers of the new faith ceased; and the growing enthusiasm of her heart gave way to more worldly impressions.

"Love, among the rest, had its share in alienating her thoughts from religion. While still very young, she became the wife of a Greek adventurer, who had come to Egypt as a purchaser of that rich tapestry, in which the needles of Persia are rivalled by the looms of the Nile. Having taken his young bride to Memphis, which was still the great mart of this merchandise, he there, in the midst of his speculations, died,—leaving his widow on the point of becoming a mother, while, as yet, but in her nineteenth year.

[177] "For single and unprotected females, it has been, at all times, a favourite resource, to seek admission into the service of some of those great temples, which absorb so much of the wealth and power of Egypt. In most of these institutions there exists an order of Priestesses, which, though not hereditary, like that of the Priests, is provided for by ample endowments, and confers that rank and station, with which, in a government so theocratic, Religion is sure to invest even her humblest handmaids. From the general policy of the Sacred College of Memphis, it may be concluded, that an accomplished female, like Theora, found but little difficulty in being chosen one of the Priestesses of Isis; and it was in the service of the subterranean shrines that her ministry chiefly lay.

"Here, a month or two after her admission, she gave birth to Alethe, who first opened her eyes among the unholy pomps and specious miracles of this mysterious region. Though Theora, as we have seen, had been diverted by other feelings from her first enthusiasm for the Christian faith, she had never wholly forgot the impression then made upon her. The sacred volume, which [178] the pious Catechumen had given her, was still treasured with care; and, though she seldom opened its pages, there was an idea of sanctity associated with it in her memory, and often would she sit to look upon it with reverential pleasure, recalling the happiness she felt when it was first made her own.

"The leisure of her new retreat, and the lone melancholy of widowhood, led her still more frequently to indulge in such thoughts, and to recur to those consoling truths which she had heard in the school of Alexandria. She now began to peruse eagerly the sacred book, drinking deep of the fountain of which she before but tasted, and feeling—what thousands of mourners, since her, have felt—that Christianity is the true religion of the sorrowful.

"This study of her secret hours became still more dear to her, from the peril with which, at that period, it was attended, and the necessity she was under of concealing from those around her the precious light that had been kindled in her heart. Too timid [179] to encounter the fierce persecution, which awaited all who were suspected of a leaning to Christianity, she continued to officiate in the pomps and ceremonies of the Temple;—though, often, with such remorse of soul, that she would pause, in the midst of the rites, and pray inwardly to God, that he would forgive this profanation of his Spirit.

"In the mean time her daughter, the young Alethe, grew up still lovelier than herself, and added, every hour, to her happiness and her fears. When arrived at a sufficient age, she was taught, like the other children of the priestesses, to take a share in the service and ceremonies of the shrines. The duty of some of these young servitors was to look after the flowers for the altar;—of others, to take care that the sacred vases were filled every day with fresh water from the Nile. The task of some was to preserve, in perfect polish, those silver images of the moon which the priests carried [180] in processions; while others were, as we have seen, employed in feeding the consecrated animals, and in keeping their plumes and scales bright, for the admiring eyes of their worshippers.

"The office allotted to Alethe—the most honourable of these minor ministries—was to wait upon the sacred birds of the Moon, to feed them with those eggs from the Nile which they loved, and provide for their use that purest water, which alone these delicate birds will touch. This employment was the delight of her childish hours; and that ibis, which Alciphron (the Epicurean) saw her dance round in the Temple, was her favourite, of all the sacred flock, and had been daily fondled and fed by her from infancy.

"Music, as being one of the chief spells of this enchanted region, was an accomplishment required of all its ministrants; and the harp, the lyre, and the sacred flute, sounded nowhere so [181] sweetly as that through these subterranean gardens. The chief object, indeed, in the education of the youth of the Temple, was to fit them, by every grace of art and nature, to give effect to the illusion of those shows and phantasms, in which the whole charm and secret of Initiation lay.

"Among the means employed to support the old system of superstition, against the infidelity and, still more, the new Faith that menaced it, was an increased display of splendour and marvels in those Mysteries for which Egypt has so long been celebrated. Of these ceremonies so many imitations had, under various names, been multiplied through Europe, that the parent superstition ran a risk of being eclipsed by its progeny; and, in order still to retain their rank of the first Priesthood in the world, those of Egypt found it necessary to continue still the best impostors.

"Accordingly, every contrivance that art could devise, or [182] labour execute—every resource that the wonderful knowledge of the Priests, in pyrotechny, mechanics, and dioptrics, could command, was brought into action to heighten the effect of their Mysteries, and give an air of enchantment to every thing connected with them.

"The final scene of beatification—the Elysium, into which the Initiate was received,—formed, of course, the leading attraction of these ceremonies; and to render it captivating alike to the

senses of the man of pleasure, and the imagination of the spiritu-
alist, was the object to which the whole skill and attention of the
Sacred College were devoted. By the influence of the Priests of
Memphis over those of the other Temples they had succeeded in
extending their subterranean frontier, both to the north and south,
so as to include, within their ever-lighted Paradise, some of the
gardens excavated for the use of the other Twelve Shrines.

"The beauty of the young Alethe, the touching sweetness of
her voice, and the sensibility that breathed throughout her every [183]
look and movement, rendered her a powerful auxiliary in such
appeals to the imagination. She was, accordingly, from her
childhood, selected from among her fair companions, as the most
worthy representative of spiritual loveliness, in those pictures of
Elysium—those scenes of another world—by which not only the
fancy, but the reason, of the excited Aspirants was dazzled.

"To the innocent child herself these shows were pastime. But
to Theora, who knew too well the imposition to which they
were subservient, this profanation of all that she loved was a
perpetual source of horror and remorse. Often would she—when
Alethe stood smiling before her, arrayed, perhaps, as a spirit of
the Elysian world,—turn away, with a shudder, from the happy
child, almost fancying that she already saw the shadows of sin
descending over that innocent brow, as she gazed on it. [184]

"As the intellect of the young maid became more active and
inquiring, the apprehensions and difficulties of the mother increased. Afraid to communicate her own precious secret, lest she
should involve her child in the dangers that encompassed it, she
yet felt it to be no less a cruelty than a crime to leave her wholly
immersed in the darkness of Paganism. In this dilemma, the
only resource that remained to her was to select, and disengage
from the dross that surrounded them, those pure particles of truth
which lie at the bottom of all religions;—those feelings, rather
than doctrines, which God has never left his creatures without,
and which, in all ages, have furnished, to those who sought it,

some clue to his glory.

"The unity and perfect goodness of the Creator; the fall of the human soul into corruption; its struggles with the darkness of this world, and its final redemption and re-ascent to the source of all spirit;—these natural solutions of the problem of our existence, these elementary grounds of all religion and virtue, which Theora had heard illustrated by her Christian teacher, lay also, she knew, veiled under the theology of Egypt; and to impress them, in all their abstract purity, upon the mind of her susceptible pupil, was, in default of more heavenly lights, her sole ambition and care.

"It was their habit, after devoting their mornings to the service of the Temple, to pass their evenings and nights in one of those small mansions above ground, allotted to some of the most favoured Priestesses, in the precincts of the Sacred College. Here, out of the reach of those gross superstitions, which pursued them, at every step, below, she endeavoured to inform, as far as she might, the mind of her beloved girl; and found it lean as naturally and instinctively to truth, as plants that have been long shut up in darkness will, when light is let in, incline themselves to its ray.

"Frequently, as they sat together on the terrace at night, contemplating that assembly of glorious stars, whose beauty first misled mankind into idolatry, she would explain to the young listener by what gradations it was that the worship, thus transferred from the Creator to the creature, sunk lower and lower in the scale of being, till man, at length, presumed to deify man, and by the most monstrous of inversions, heaven was made the mirror of earth, reflecting all its most earthly features.

"Even in the Temple itself, the anxious mother would endeavour to interpose her purer lessons among the idolatrous ceremonies in which they were engaged. When the favourite ibis of Alethe took its station on the shrine, and the young maiden was seen approaching, with all the gravity of worship, the very bird which she had played with but an hour before,—when the

[185]
[186]

acacia-bough, which she herself had plucked, seemed to acquire a sudden sacredness in her eyes, as soon as the priest had breathed [187] on it,—on all such occasions Theora, though with fear and trembling, would venture to suggest to the youthful worshipper the distinction that should be drawn between the sensible object of adoration, and that spiritual, unseen Deity, of which it was but the remembrancer or type.

"With sorrow, however, she soon discovered that, in thus but partially enlightening a mind too ardent to be satisfied with such glimmerings, she only bewildered the heart that she meant to guide, and cut down the hope round which its faith twined, without substituting any other support in its place. As the beauty, too, of Alethe began to attract all eyes, new fears crowded upon the mother's heart;—fears, in which she was but too much justified by the characters of some of those around her.

"In this sacred abode, as may easily be conceived, morality did not always go hand in hand with religion. The hypocritical [188] and ambitious Orcus, who was, at this period, High Priest of Memphis, was a man, in every respect, qualified to preside over a system of such splendid fraud. He had reached that effective time of life, when enough of the warmth of youth remains to give animation to the counsels of age. But, in his instance, youth had only the baser passions to bequeath, while age but contributed a more refined maturity of mischief. The advantages of a faith appealing so wholly to the senses, were well understood by him; nor was he ignorant that the only way of making religion subservient to his own interests was by shaping it adroitly to the passions of others.

"The state of misery and remorse in which the mind of Theora was kept by the scenes, however veiled by hypocrisy, which she witnessed around her, became at length intolerable. No perils that the cause of truth could bring with it would be half so dreadful [189] as this endurance of sinfulness and deceit. Her child was, as yet, pure and innocent;—but, without that sentinel of the soul,

Religion, how long might she continue so?

"This thought at once decided her;—all other fears vanished before it. She resolved instantly to lay open to Alethe the whole secret of her soul; to make her, who was her only hope on earth, the sharer of all her hopes in heaven, and then fly with her, as soon as possible, from this unhallowed place, to the desert—to the mountains—to any place, however desolate, where God and the consciousness of innocence might be with them.

"The promptitude with which her young pupil caught from her the divine truths, was even beyond what she expected. It was like the lighting of one torch at another,—so prepared was Alethe's mind for the illumination. Amply was the mother now repaid for all her misery, by this perfect communion of love and faith, and by the delight with which she saw her beloved child—like the young antelope, when first led by her dam to the well,—drink thirstily by her side, at the source of all life and truth.

"But such happiness was not long to last. The anxieties that Theora had suffered preyed upon her health. She felt her strength daily decline; and the thoughts of leaving, alone and unguarded in the world, that treasure which she had just devoted to heaven, gave her a feeling of despair which but hastened the ebb of life. Had she put in practice her resolution of flying from this place, her child might have been now beyond the reach of all she dreaded, and in the solitude of the wilderness would have found at least safety from wrong. But the very happiness she had felt in her new task diverted her from this project;—and it was now too late, for she was already dying.

"She concealed, however, her state from the tender and sanguine girl, who, though she saw the traces of disease on her mother's cheek, little knew that they were the hastening footsteps of death, nor thought even of the possibility of losing what was so dear to her. Too soon, however, the moment of separation arrived; and while the anguish and dismay of Alethe were in proportion to the security in which she had indulged, Theora,

[190]

[191]

too, felt, with bitter regret, that she had sacrificed to her fond consideration much precious time, and that there now remained but a few brief and painful moments, for the communication of all those wishes and instructions, on which the future destiny of the young orphan depended.

"She had, indeed, time for little more than to place the sacred volume solemnly in her hands, to implore that she would, at all risks, fly from this unholy place, and, pointing in the direction of the mountains of the Saïd, to name, with her last breath, the holy [192] man, to whom, under heaven, she trusted for the protection and salvation of her child.

"The first violence of feeling to which Alethe gave way was succeeded by a fixed and tearless grief, which rendered her insensible, for some time, to the dangers of her situation. Her only comfort was in visiting that monumental chapel, where the beautiful remains of Theora lay. There, night after night, in contemplation of those placid features, and in prayers for the peace of the departed spirit, did she pass her lonely, and—sad as they were—happiest hours. Though the mystic emblems that decorated that chapel were but ill suited to the slumber of a Christian saint, there was one among them, the Cross, which, by a remarkable coincidence, is an emblem common alike to the Gentile and the Christian,—being, to the former, a shadowy type of that immortality, of which, to the latter, it is a substantial and assuring pledge. [193]

"Nightly, upon this cross, which she had often seen her lost mother kiss, did she breathe forth a solemn and heartfelt vow, never to abandon the faith which that departed spirit had bequeathed to her. To such enthusiasm, indeed, did her heart at such moments rise, that, but for the last injunctions from those pallid lips, she would, at once, have avowed her perilous secret, and spoken out the words, 'I am a Christian,' among those benighted shrines!

"But the will of her, to whom she owed more than life, was

to be obeyed. To escape from this haunt of superstition must now, she felt, be her first object; and, in devising the means of effecting it, her mind, day and night, was employed. It was with a loathing not to be concealed she now found herself compelled to resume her idolatrous services at the shrine. To some of the offices of Theora she succeeded, as is the custom, by inheritance; and in the performance of these—sanctified as they were in her eyes by the pure spirit she had seen engaged in them—there was a sort of melancholy pleasure in which her sorrow found relief. But the part she was again forced to take, in the scenic shows of the Mysteries, brought with it a sense of wrong and degradation which she could no longer bear.

[194]

"She had already formed, in her own mind, a plan of escape, in which her knowledge of all the windings of this subterranean realm gave her confidence, when the reception of Alciphron, as an Initiate, took place.

"From the first moment of the landing of that philosopher at Alexandria, he had become an object of suspicion and watchful-ness to the inquisitorial Orcus, whom philosophy, in any shape, naturally alarmed, but to whom the sect over which the young Athenian presided was particularly obnoxious. The accomplish-ments of Alciphron, his popularity, wherever he went, and the freedom with which he indulged his wit at the expense of religion, was all faithfully reported to the High Priest by his spies, and stirred up within him no kindly feelings towards the stranger. In dealing with an infidel, such a personage as Orcus could know no alternative but that of either converting or destroying him; and though his spite, as a man, would have been more gratified by the latter proceeding, his pride, as a priest, led him to prefer the triumph of the former.

[195]

"The first descent of the Epicurean into the pyramid was speedily known, and the alarm immediately given to the Priests below. As soon as it was discovered that the young philosopher of Athens was the intruder, and that he still continued to linger round the pyramid, looking often and wistfully towards the portal, it was concluded that his curiosity would impel him to try a second descent; and Orcus, blessing the good chance which had thus brought the wild bird to his net, determined not to allow an [196] opportunity so precious to be wasted.

"Instantly, the whole of that wonderful machinery, by which the phantasms and illusions of Initiation are produced, were put in active preparation throughout that subterranean realm; and the increased stir and watchfulness excited among its inmates, by this more than ordinary display of all the resources of priestcraft, rendered the accomplishment of Alethe's design, at such a moment, peculiarly difficult. Wholly ignorant of the share which had fallen to herself in attracting the young philosopher down to this region, she but heard of him vaguely, as the Chief of a great Grecian sect, who had been led, by either curiosity or accident, to expose himself to the first trials of Initiation, and whom the priests, she saw, were endeavouring to ensnare in their toils, by every art and skill with which their science of darkness had gifted them.   [197]

"To her mind, the image of a philosopher, such as Alciphron had been represented to her, came associated with ideas of age and reverence; and, more than once, the possibility of his being made instrumental to her deliverance flashed a hope across her heart in which she could not help indulging. Often had she been told by Theora of the many Gentile sages, who had laid their wisdom down humbly at the foot of the Cross; and though this Initiate, she feared, could hardly be among the number, yet the rumours which she had gathered from the servants of the Temple, of his undisguised contempt for the errors of heathenism, led her to hope she might find tolerance, if not sympathy, in her appeal to him.

"Nor was it solely with a view to her own chance of deliverance that she thus connected him in her thoughts with the plan which she meditated. The look of proud and self-gratulating mal- [198]

ice, with which the High Priest had mentioned this 'infidel,' as he styled him, when instructing her in the scene she was to enact before the philosopher in the valley, but too plainly informed her of the destiny that hung over him. She knew how many were the hapless candidates for Initiation, who had been doomed to a durance worse than that of the grave, for but a word, a whisper breathed against the sacred absurdities which they witnessed; and it was evident to her that the venerable Greek (for such her fancy represented Alciphron) was no less interested in escaping from this region than herself.

"Her own resolution was, at all events, fixed. That visionary scene, in which she had appeared before Alciphron,—little knowing how ardent were the heart and imagination, over which her beauty, at that moment, shed its whole influence,—was, she solemnly resolved, the very last unholy service, that superstition or imposture should ever command of her.

[199]

"On the following night the Aspirant was to watch in the Great Temple of Isis. Such an opportunity of approaching and addressing him might never come again. Should he, from compassion for her situation, or a sense of the danger of his own, consent to lend his aid to her flight, most gladly would she accept it,—assured that no danger or treachery she might risk could be half so dreadful as those she left behind. Should he, on the contrary, refuse, her determination was equally fixed—to trust to that God, who watches over the innocent, and go forth alone.

"To reach the island in Lake Mœris was her first object, and there occurred luckily, at this time, a mode of accomplishing it, by which the difficulty and dangers of the attempt would be, in a great degree, diminished. The day of the annual visitation of the High Priest to the Place of Weeping—as that island in the centre of the lake is called—was now fast approaching; and Alethe well knew that the self-moving car, by which the High Priest and one of the Hierophants are conveyed to the chambers under the lake, stood waiting in readiness. By availing herself of this expedient,

[200]

she would gain the double advantage both of facilitating her own flight and retarding the speed of her pursuers.

"Having paid a last visit to the tomb of her beloved mother, and wept there, long and passionately, till her heart almost failed in the struggle,—having paused, too, to give a kiss to her favourite ibis, which, though too much a Christian to worship, she was still child enough to love,—with a trembling step she went early to the Sanctuary, and hid herself in one of the recesses of the Shrine. Her intention was to steal out from thence to Alciphron, while it was yet dark, and before the illumination of the great [201] Statue behind the Veils had begun. But her fears delayed her till it was almost too late;—already was the image lighted up, and still she remained trembling in her hiding place.

"In a few minutes more the mighty Veils would have been withdrawn, and the glories of that scene of enchantment laid open,—when, at length, summoning up courage, and taking advantage of a momentary absence of those employed in the preparations of this splendid mockery, she stole from under the Veil and found her way, through the gloom, to the Epicurean. There was then no time for explanation;—she had but to trust to the simple words, 'Follow, and be silent;' and the implicit readiness with which she found them obeyed filled her with no less surprise than the philosopher himself felt in hearing them.

"In a second or two they were on their way through the sub-terranean windings, leaving the ministers of Isis to waste their [202] splendours on vacancy, through a long series of miracles and visions which they now exhibited,—unconscious that he, whom they took such pains to dazzle, was already, under the guidance of the young Christian, removed beyond the reach of their spells."

CHAP. XIV.

Such was the story, of which this innocent girl gave me, in her own touching language, the outline.

The sun was just rising as she finished her narrative. Fearful of encountering the expression of those feelings with which, she could not but observe, I was affected by her recital, scarcely had she concluded the last sentence, when, rising abruptly from her seat, she hurried into the pavilion, leaving me with the words already crowding for utterance to my lips.

Oppressed by the various emotions, thus sent back upon my heart, I lay down on the deck in a state of agitation, that defied even the most distant approaches of sleep. While every word she had uttered, every feeling she expressed, but ministered new fuel to that flame within me, to describe which, passion is too weak a word, there was also much of her recital that disheartened, that alarmed me. To find a Christian thus under the garb of a Memphian Priestess, was a discovery that, had my heart been less deeply interested, would but have more powerfully stimulated my imagination and pride. But, when I recollected the austerity of the faith she had embraced,—the tender and sacred tie, associated with it in her memory, and the devotion of woman's heart to objects thus consecrated,—her very perfections but widened the distance between us, and all that most kindled my passion at the same time chilled my hopes.

Were we left to each other, as on this silent river, in this undisturbed communion of thoughts and feelings, I knew too well, I thought, both her sex's nature and my own, to feel a doubt that love would ultimately triumph. But the severity of the guardianship to which I must resign her,—some monk of the desert, some stern Solitary,—the influence such a monitor would gain over her mind, and the horror with which, ere long, she would be taught to regard the reprobate infidel on whom she now smiled,—in all this prospect I saw nothing but despair. After a few short hours, my happiness would be at an end, and such a dark chasm open between our fates, as must sever them, far as earth is from heaven, asunder. [205]

It was true, she was now wholly in my power. I feared no witnesses but those of earth, and the solitude of the desert was at hand. But though I acknowledged not a heaven, I worshipped her who was, to me, its type and substitute. If, at any moment, a single thought of wrong or deceit, towards a creature so sacred, arose in my mind, one look from her innocent eyes averted the sacrilege. Even passion itself felt a holy fear in her presence,—like the flame trembling in the breeze of the sanctuary,—and Love, pure Love, stood in place of Religion. [206]

As long as I knew not her story, I might indulge, at least, in dreams of the future. But, now—what hope, what prospect remained? My sole chance of happiness lay in the feeble hope of beguiling away her thoughts from the plan which she meditated; of weaning her, by persuasion, from that austere faith, which I had before hated and now feared, and of—attaching her, perhaps, alone and unlinked as she was in the world, to my own fortunes for ever!

In the agitation of these thoughts, I had started from my rest-ing-place, and continued to pace up and down, under a burning sun, till, exhausted both by thought and feeling, I sunk down, amid its blaze, into a sleep, which, to my fevered brain, seemed a sleep of fire.

On awaking, I found the veil of Alethe laid carefully over my brow, while she, herself, sat near me, under the shadow of the sail, looking anxiously at that leaf, which her mother had given [207] her, and apparently employed in comparing its outlines with the course of the river and the forms of the rocky hills by which we passed. She looked pale and troubled, and rose eagerly to meet me, as if she had long and impatiently waited for my waking.

Her heart, it was plain, had been disturbed from its security, and was beginning to take alarm at its own feelings. But, though vaguely conscious of the peril to which she was exposed, her reliance, as is usually the case, increased with her danger, and on me, far more than on herself, did she depend for saving her from it. To reach, as soon as possible, her asylum in the desert, was now the urgent object of her entreaties and wishes; and the self-reproach she expressed at having permitted her thoughts to be diverted, for a single moment, from this sacred purpose, not only revealed the truth, that she had forgotten it, but betrayed even a glimmering consciousness of the cause.

[208]

Her sleep, she said, had been broken by ill-omened dreams. Every moment the shade of her mother had stood before her, rebuking her, with mournful looks, for her delay, and pointing, as she had done in death, to the eastern hills. Bursting into tears at this accusing recollection, she hastily placed the leaf, which she had been examining, in my hands, and implored that I would ascertain, without a moment's delay, what portion of our voyage was still unperformed, and in what space of time we might hope to accomplish it.

I had, still less than herself, taken note of either place or distance; and, had we been left to glide on in this dream of happiness, should never have thought of pausing to ask where it would end. But such confidence, I felt, was too sacred to be deceived. Reluctant as I was, naturally, to enter on an inquiry, which might so soon dissipate even my last hope, her wish was sufficient to supersede even the selfishness of love, and on the instant I proceeded to obey her will.

[209]

There is, on the eastern bank of the Nile, to the north of Antinöe, a high and steep rock, impending over the flood, which for ages, from a prodigy connected with it, has borne the name of the Mountain of the Birds. Yearly, it is said, at a certain season and hour, large flocks of birds assemble in the ravine, of which this rocky mountain forms one of the sides, and are there observed to go through the mysterious ceremony of inserting each its beak into a particular cleft of the rock, till the cleft closes upon one of their number, when the rest, taking wing, leave the selected victim to die.

Through the ravine where this charm—for such the multitude consider it—is worked, there ran, in ancient times, a canal from the Nile, to some great and forgotten city that now lies buried [210] in the desert. To a short distance from the river this canal still exists, but, soon after having passed through the defile, its scanty waters disappear altogether, and are lost under the sands.

It was in the neighbourhood of this place, as I could collect from the delineations on the leaf,—where a flight of birds represented the name of the mountain,—that the dwelling of the Solitary, to whom Alethe was bequeathed, lay. Imperfect as was my knowledge of the geography of Egypt, it at once struck me, that we had long since left this mountain behind; and, on inquiring of our boatmen, I found my conjecture confirmed. We had, indeed, passed it, as appeared, on the preceding night; and, as the wind had, ever since, blown strongly from the north, and the sun was already declining towards the horizon, we must now be, at least, an ordinary day's sail to the southward of the spot. [211]

At this discovery, I own, my heart felt a joy which I could with difficulty conceal. It seemed to me as if fortune was conspiring with love, and, by thus delaying the moment of our separation, afforded me at least a chance of happiness. Her look, too, and manner, when informed of our mistake, rather encouraged than chilled this secret hope. In the first moment of astonishment, her eyes opened upon me with a suddenness of splendour, under which I felt my own wink, as if lightning had crossed them. But she again, as suddenly, let their lids fall, and, after a quiver of her lip, which showed the conflict of feeling within, crossed her arms upon her bosom, and looked silently down upon the deck;—her whole countenance sinking into an expression, sad, but resigned, as if she felt, with me, that fate was on the side of wrong, and saw Love already stealing between her soul and heaven.

[212] I was not slow in availing myself of what I fancied to be the irresolution of her mind. But, fearful of exciting alarm by any appeal to tenderer feelings, I but addressed myself to her imagination, and to that love of novelty, which is for ever fresh in the youthful breast. We were now approaching that region of wonders, Thebes. "In a day or two," said I, "we shall see, towering above the waters, the colossal Avenue of Sphinxes, and the bright Obelisks of the Sun. We shall visit the plain of Memnon, and those mighty statues, that fling their shadows at sunrise over the Libyan hills. We shall hear the image of the Son of the Morning answering to the first touch of light. From thence, in a few hours, a breeze like this will transport us to those sunny islands near the cataracts; there, to wander, among the sacred palm-groves of Philæ, or sit, at noon-tide hour, in those cool alcoves, which the waterfall of Syene shadows under its arch.

[213] Oh, who, with such scenes of loveliness within reach, would turn coldly away to the bleak desert, and leave this fair world, with all its enchantments, shining behind them, unseen and unenjoyed? At least,"—I added, tenderly taking her by the hand,—"at least, let a few more days be stolen from the dreary fate to which thou hast devoted thyself, and then——"

She had heard but the last few words;—the rest had been lost upon her. Startled by the tone of tenderness, into which, in spite of all my resolves, my voice had softened, she looked for an instant in my face, with passionate earnestness;—then, dropping upon her knees with her clasped hands upraised, exclaimed—"Tempt me not, in the name of God I implore thee, tempt me not to swerve from my sacred duty. Oh, take me instantly to that desert mountain, and I will bless thee for ever."

This appeal, I felt, *could not* be resisted,—though my heart were to break for it. Having silently expressed my assent to her prayer, by a pressure of her hand as I raised her from the [214] deck, I hastened, as we were still in full career for the south, to give orders that our sail should be instantly lowered, and not a moment lost in retracing our course.

In proceeding, however, to give these directions, it, for the first time, occurred to me, that, as I had hired this yacht in the neighbourhood of Memphis, where it was probable that the flight of the young fugitive would be most vigilantly tracked, we should act imprudently in betraying to the boatmen the place of her re-treat;—and the present seemed the most favourable opportunity of evading such a danger. Desiring, therefore, that we should be landed at a small village on the shore, under pretence of paying a visit to some shrine in the neighbourhood, I there dismissed our barge, and was relieved from fear of further observation, by seeing it again set sail, and resume its course fleetly up the current.   [215]

From the boats of all descriptions that lay idle beside the bank, I now selected one, which, in every respect, suited my purpose,—being, in its shape and accommodations, a miniature of our former vessel, but so small and light as to be manageable by myself alone, and, with the advantage of the current, requiring little more than a hand to steer it. This boat I succeeded, with-out much difficulty, in purchasing, and, after a short delay, we were again afloat down the current;—the sun just then sinking, in conscious glory, over his own golden shrines in the Libyan waste.

The evening was more calm and lovely than any that yet had smiled upon our voyage; and, as we left the bank, there came soothingly over our ears a strain of sweet, rustic melody from the shore. It was the voice of a young Nubian girl, whom we saw kneeling on the bank before an acacia, and singing, while her companions stood round, the wild song of invocation, which, in   [216] her country, they address to that enchanted tree:—

> "Oh! Abyssinian tree,
>   We pray, we pray, to thee;
> By the glow of thy golden fruit,
>   And the violet hue of thy flower,
>   And the greeting mute
>   Of thy bough's salute
> To the stranger who seeks thy bower.[6]

II.

> "Oh! Abyssinian tree,
>   How the traveller blesses thee,
> When the night no moon allows,
>   And the sun-set hour is near,
>   And thou bend'st thy boughs
>   To kiss his brows,
> Saying, 'Come rest thee here.'
>   Oh! Abyssinian tree,
>   Thus bow thy head to me!"

[217]

In the burden of this song the companions of the young Nubian joined; and we heard the words, "Oh! Abyssinian tree," dying away on the breeze, long after the whole group had been lost to our eyes.

Whether, in this new arrangement which I had made for our voyage, any motive, besides those which I professed, had a share, I can scarcely, even myself, so bewildered were my feelings, determine. But no sooner had the current borne us away from all human dwellings, and we were alone on the waters, with not a soul near, than I felt how closely such solitude draws hearts together, and how much more we seemed to belong to each other, than when there were eyes around.

---

[6] See an account of this sensitive tree, which bends down its branches to those who approach it, in M. Jomard's Description of Syene and the Cataracts.

The same feeling, but without the same sense of its danger, was manifest in every look and word of Alethe. The consciousness of the one great effort she had made appeared to have satisfied her heart on the score of duty,—while the devotedness with which she saw I attended to her every wish, was felt with [218] all that gratitude which, in woman, is the day-spring of love. She was, therefore, happy, innocently happy; and the confiding, and even affectionate, unreserve of her manner, while it rendered my trust more sacred, made it also far more difficult.

It was only, however, on subjects unconnected with our situation or fate, that she yielded to such interchange of thought, or that her voice ventured to answer mine. The moment I alluded to the destiny that awaited us, all her cheerfulness fled, and she became saddened and silent. When I described to her the beauty of my own native land—its founts of inspiration and fields of glory—her eyes sparkled with sympathy, and sometimes even softened into fondness. But when I ventured to whisper, that, in that glorious country, a life full of love and liberty awaited her; when I proceeded to contrast the adoration and bliss she might [219] command, with the gloomy austerities of the life to which she was hastening,—it was like the coming of a sudden cloud over a summer sky. Her head sunk, as she listened;—I waited in vain for an answer; and when, half playfully reproaching her for this silence, I stooped to take her hand, I could feel the warm tears fast falling over it.

But even this—little hope as it held out—was happiness. Though it foreboded that I should lose her, it also whispered that I was loved. Like that lake, in the Land of Roses[7], whose waters are half sweet, half bitter, I felt my fate to be a compound of bliss and pain,—but the very pain well worth all ordinary bliss.

And thus did the hours of that night pass along; while every moment shortened our happy dream, and the current seemed to

[7] The province of Arsinoë, now Fioum.

[220]

flow with a swifter pace than any that ever yet hurried to the sea. Not a feature of the whole scene but is, at this moment, freshly in my memory;—the broken star-light on the water;—the rippling sound of the boat, as, without oar or sail, it went, like a thing of enchantment, down the stream;—the scented fire, burning beside us on the deck, and, oh, that face, on which its light fell, still revealing, as it turned, some new charm, some blush or look, more beautiful than the last.

Often, while I sat gazing, forgetful of all else in this world, our boat, left wholly to itself, would drive from its course, and, bearing us to the bank, get entangled in the water-flowers, or be caught in some eddy, ere I perceived where we were. Once, too, when the rustling of my oar among the flowers had startled away from the bank some wild antelopes, that had stolen, at that still hour, to drink of the Nile, what an emblem I thought it of

[221]

the young heart beside me,—tasting, for the first time, of hope and love, and so soon, alas, to be scared from their sweetness for ever!

CHAP. XV.

The night was now far advanced;—the bend of our course to-wards the left, and the closing in of the eastern hills upon the river, gave warning of our approach to the hermit's dwelling. Every minute now seemed like the last of existence; and I felt a sinking of despair at my heart, which would have been intolerable, had not a resolution that suddenly, and as if by inspiration, occurred to me, presented a glimpse of hope which, in some degree, calmed my feelings.

Much as I had, all my life, despised hypocrisy,—the very sect I had embraced being chiefly recommended to me by the war which they waged on the cant of all others,—it was, nevertheless, in hypocrisy that I now scrupled not to take refuge from, what I [223] dreaded more than shame or death, my separation from Alethe. In my despair, I adopted the humiliating plan—deeply humiliating as I felt it to be, even amid the joy with which I welcomed it—of offering myself to this hermit, as a convert to his faith, and thus becoming the fellow-disciple of Alethe under his care!

From the moment I resolved upon this plan, my spirit felt lightened. Though having fully before my eyes the labyrinth of imposture into which it would lead me, I thought of nothing but the chance of our being still together;—in this hope, all pride, all philosophy was forgotten, and every thing seemed tolerable, but the prospect of losing her.

Thus resolved, it was with somewhat less reluctant feelings, that I now undertook, at the anxious desire of Alethe, to ascertain the site of that well-known mountain, in the neighbourhood

of which the dwelling of the anchoret lay. We had already [224
passed one or two stupendous rocks, which stood, detached, like
fortresses, over the river's brink, and which, in some degree,
corresponded with the description on the leaf. So little was there
of life now stirring along the shores, that I had begun almost
to despair of any assistance from inquiry, when, on looking to
the western bank, I saw a boatman among the sedges, towing
his small boat, with some difficulty, up the current. Hailing
him, as we passed, I asked, "Where stands the Mountain of
the Birds?"—and he had hardly time to answer, pointing above
our heads, "There," when we perceived that we were just then
entering into the shadow, which this mighty rock flings across
the whole of the flood.

In a few moments we had reached the mouth of the ravine,
of which the Mountain of the Birds forms one of the sides, and
through which the scanty canal from the Nile flows. At the sight
[225] of this chasm, in some of whose gloomy recesses—if we had
rightly interpreted the leaf—the dwelling of the Solitary lay, our
voices, at once, sunk into a low whisper, while Alethe looked
round upon me with a superstitious fearfulness, as if doubtful
whether I had not already disappeared from her side. A quick
movement, however, of her hand towards the ravine, told too
plainly that her purpose was still unchanged. With my oars,
therefore, checking the career of our boat, I succeeded, after no
small exertion, in turning it out of the current of the river, and
steering into this bleak and stagnant canal.

Our transition from life and bloom to the very depth of desolation, was immediate. While the water and one side of the ravine
lay buried in shadow, the white, skeleton-like crags of the other
stood aloft in the pale glare of moonlight. The sluggish stream
through which we moved, yielded sullenly to the oar, and the
[226] shriek of a few water-birds, which we had roused from their fast-
nesses, was succeeded by a silence, so dead and awful, that our
lips seemed afraid to disturb it by a breath; and half-whispered

exclamations, "How dreary!"—"How dismal!"—were almost the only words exchanged between us.

We had proceeded for some time through this gloomy defile, when, at a distance before us, among the rocks on which the moonlight fell, we perceived, upon a ledge but little elevated above the canal, a small hut or cave, which, from a tree or two planted around it, had some appearance of being the abode of a human being. "This, then," thought I, "is the home to which Alethe is destined!"—A chill of despair came again over my heart, and the oars, as I gazed, lay motionless in my hands.

I found Alethe, too, whose eyes had caught the same object, drawing closer to my side than she had yet ventured. Laying her hand agitatedly upon mine, "We must here," she said, "part [227] for ever." I turned to her, as she spoke: there was a tenderness, a despondency in her countenance, that at once saddened and inflamed my soul. "Part!" I exclaimed passionately,—"No!—the same God shall receive us both. Thy faith, Alethe, shall, from this hour, be mine, and I will live and die in this desert with thee!"

Her surprise, her delight, at these words, was like a momentary delirium. The wild, anxious smile, with which she looked into my face, as if to ascertain whether she had, indeed, heard my words aright, bespoke a happiness too much for reason to bear. At length the fulness of her heart found relief in tears; and, murmuring forth an incoherent blessing on my name, she let her head fall languidly and powerlessly on my arm. The light from our boat-fire shone upon her face. I saw her eyes, which she had closed for a moment, again opening upon me with the same [228] tenderness, and—merciful Providence, how I remember that moment!—was on the point of bending down my lips towards hers, when, suddenly, in the air above our heads, as if it came from heaven, there burst forth a strain from a choir of voices, that with its solemn sweetness filled the whole valley.

Breaking away from my caress at these supernatural sounds,

the maiden threw herself trembling upon her knees, and, not daring to look up, exclaimed wildly, "My mother, oh my mother!"

It was the Christian's morning hymn that we heard;—the same,
as I learned afterwards, that, on their high terrace at Memphis,
Alethe had been often taught by her mother to sing to the rising
sun.

Scarcely less startled than my companion, I looked up, and,
at the very summit of the rock above us, saw a light, appearing
to come from a small opening or window, through which also
the sounds, that had appeared so supernatural, issued. There
could be no doubt, that we had now found—if not the dwelling
of the anchoret—at least, the haunt of some of the Christian
brotherhood of these rocks, by whose assistance we could not
fail to find the place of his retreat.

The agitation, into which Alethe had been thrown by the first
burst of that psalmody, soon yielded to the softening recollections
which it brought back; and a calm came over her brow, such as
it had never before worn, since our meeting. She seemed to feel
that she had now reached her destined haven, and to hail, as the
voice of heaven itself, those sounds by which she was welcomed
to it.

In her tranquillity, however, I could not now sympathize.
Impatient to know all that awaited her and myself, I pushed our
boat close to the base of the rock,—directly under that lighted
window on the summit, to find my way up to which was my first
object. Having hastily received my instructions from Alethe,
and made her repeat again the name of the Christian whom we
sought, I sprang upon the bank, and was not long in discovering
a sort of rude stair-way, cut out of the rock, but leading, I found,
by easy windings, up the steep.

After ascending for some time, I arrived at a level space or
ledge, which the hand of labour had succeeded in converting into
a garden, and which was planted, here and there, with fig-trees
and palms. Around it, too, I could perceive, through the glim-

[229]

[230]

mering light, a number of small caves or grottos, into some of which, human beings might find entrance, while others appeared no larger than the tombs of the Sacred Birds round Lake Mœris.

I was still, I found, but half-way up the ascent to the summit, nor could perceive any further means of continuing my course, as the mountain from hence rose, almost perpendicularly, like a wall. At length, however, on exploring around, I discovered behind the shade of a sycamore a large ladder of wood, resting [231] firmly against the rock, and affording an easy and secure ascent up the steep.

Having ascertained thus far, I again descended to the boat for Alethe,—whom I found trembling already at her short solitude,—and having led her up the steps to this quiet garden, left her safely lodged, amid its holy silence, while I pursued my way upward to the light on the rock.

At the top of the long ladder I found myself on another ledge or platform, somewhat smaller than the first, but planted in the same manner, with trees, and, as I could perceive by the mingled light of morning and the moon, embellished with flowers. I was now near the summit;—there remained but another short ascent, and, as a ladder against the rock, as before, supplied the means of scaling it, I was in a few minutes at the opening from which the light issued.

I had ascended gently, as well from a feeling of awe at the [232] whole scene, as from an unwillingness to disturb too rudely the rites on which I intruded. My approach was, therefore, unheard, and an opportunity, during some moments, afforded me of observing the group within, before my appearance at the window was discovered.

In the middle of the apartment, which seemed once to have been a Pagan oratory, there was an assembly of seven or eight persons, some male, some female, kneeling in silence round a small altar;—while, among them, as if presiding over their ceremony, stood an aged man, who, at the moment of my arrival, was presenting to one of the female worshippers an alabaster cup, which she applied, with much reverence, to her lips. On the countenance of the venerable minister, as he pronounced a short prayer over her head, there was an expression of profound feeling that showed how wholly he was absorbed in that rite; and when she had drank of the cup,—which I saw had engraven on its side the image of a head, with a glory round it,—the holy man bent down and kissed her forehead.

[233]

After this parting salutation, the whole group rose silently from their knees; and it was then, for the first time, that, by a cry of terror from one of the women, the appearance of a stranger at the window was discovered. The whole assembly seemed startled and alarmed, except him, that superior person, who, advancing from the altar, with an unmoved look, raised the latch of the door, which was adjoining to the window, and admitted me.

There was, in this old man's features, a mixture of elevation and sweetness, of simplicity and energy, which commanded at once attachment and homage; and half hoping, half fearing to find in him the destined guardian of Alethe, I looked anxiously in his face, as I entered, and pronounced the name "Melanius!" "Melanius is my name, young stranger," he answered; "and whether in friendship or in enmity thou comest, Melanius blesses thee." Thus saying, he made a sign with his right hand above my head, while, with involuntary respect, I bowed beneath the benediction.

[234]

"Let this volume," I replied, "answer for the peacefulness of my mission,"—at the same time, placing in his hands the copy of the Scriptures, which had been his own gift to the mother of Alethe, and which her child now brought as the credential of her claims on his protection. At the sight of this sacred pledge, which he recognized instantly, the solemnity that had marked his first reception of me softened into tenderness. Thoughts of other times seemed to pass through his mind, and as, with a sigh of recollection, he took the book from my hands, some words on the outer leaf caught his eye. They were few,—but contained, perhaps, the last wishes of the dying Theora, for as he eagerly read them over, I saw the tears in his aged eyes. "The trust," [235] he said, with a faltering voice, "is sacred, and God will, I hope, enable his servant to guard it faithfully."

During this short dialogue, the other persons of the assembly had departed—being, as I afterwards learned, brethren from the neighbouring bank of the Nile, who came thus secretly before day-break, to join in worshipping God. Fearful lest their descent down the rock might alarm Alethe, I hurried briefly over the few words of explanation that remained, and, leaving the venerable Christian to follow at his leisure, hastened anxiously down to rejoin the maiden.

CHAP. XVI.

Melanius was among the first of those Christians of Egypt, who, after the recent example of the hermit, Paul, renouncing all the comforts of social existence, betook themselves to a life of contemplation in the desert. Less selfish, however, in his piety, than most of these ascetics, Melanius forgot not the world, in leaving it. He knew that man was not born to live wholly for himself; that his relation to human kind was that of the link to the chain, and that even his solitude should be turned to the advantage of others. In flying, therefore, from the din and disturbance of life, he sought not to place himself beyond the reach of its sympathies, but selected a retreat, where he could combine the advantage of solitude with those opportunities of serving his fellow-men, which a neighbourhood to their haunts would afford.

That taste for the gloom of subterranean recesses, which the race of Misraim inherit from their Ethiopian ancestors, had, by hollowing out all Egypt into caverns and crypts, furnished these Christian anchorets with a choice of retreats. Accordingly, some found a shelter in the grottos of Elethya;—others, among the royal tombs of the Thebaïd. In the middle of the Seven Valleys, where the sun rarely shines, a few have fixed their dim and melancholy retreat, while others have sought the neighbourhood of the red Lakes of Nitria, and there,—like those Pagan solitaries of old, who dwelt among the palm-trees near the Dead Sea,—muse amid the sterility of nature, and seem to find, in her desolation, peace.

It was on one of the mountains of the Saïd, to the east of the river, that Melanius, as we have seen, chose his place of seclusion,—between the life and fertility of the Nile on the one side, and the lone, dismal barrenness of the desert on the other. Half-way down this mountain, where it impends over the ravine, he found a series of caves or grottos dug out of the rock, which had, in other times, ministered to some purpose of mystery, but whose use had been long forgotten, and their recesses abandoned.

To this place, after the banishment of his great master, Origen, Melanius, with a few faithful followers, retired, and, by the example of his innocent life, no less than by his fervid eloquence, succeeded in winning crowds of converts to his faith. Placed, as he was, in the neighbourhood of the rich city, Antinoë, though he mingled not with its multitude, his name and his fame were among them, and, to all who sought instruction or consolation, the cell of the hermit was ever open.

Notwithstanding the rigid abstinence of his own habits, he [239] was yet careful to provide for the comforts of others. Contented with a rude bed of straw, himself, for the stranger he had always a less homely resting-place. From his grotto, the wayfaring and the indigent never went unrefreshed; and, with the assistance of some of his brethren, he had formed gardens along the ledges of the mountain, which gave an air of cheerfulness to his rocky dwelling, and supplied him with the chief necessaries of such a climate, fruit and shade.

Though the acquaintance which he had formed with the mother of Alethe, during the short period of her attendance at the school of Origen, was soon interrupted, and never afterwards renewed, the interest which he had then taken in her fate was too lively to be forgotten. He had seen the zeal with which her young heart welcomed instruction; and the thought that such a candidate for heaven should have relapsed into idolatry, came often, with disquieting apprehension, over his mind. [240]

It was, therefore, with true pleasure, that, but a year or two before her death, he had learned, by a private communication from Theora, transmitted through a Christian embalmer of Memphis, that "not only her own heart had taken root in the faith, but that a new bud had flowered with the same divine hope, and that, ere long, he might see them both transplanted to the desert."

The coming, therefore, of Alethe was far less a surprise to him, than her coming thus alone was a shock and a sorrow; and the silence of their meeting showed how deeply each remembered that the tie which had brought them together was no longer of this world,—that the hand, which should have been joined with theirs, was in the tomb. I now saw that not even religion was proof against the sadness of mortality. For, as the old man put the [241] ringlets aside from her forehead, and contemplated in that clear countenance the reflection of what her mother had been, there was a mournfulness mingled with his piety, as he said, "Heaven rest her soul!" which showed how little even the certainty of a heaven for those we love can subdue our regret for having lost them on earth.

The full light of day had now risen upon the desert, and our host, reminded, by the faint looks of Alethe, of the many anxious hours we had passed without sleep, proposed that we should seek, in the chambers of the rock, such rest as the dwelling of a hermit could offer. Pointing to one of the largest openings, as he addressed me,—"Thou wilt find," he said, "in that grotto a bed of fresh doum leaves, and may the consciousness of having protected the orphan sweeten thy sleep!"

I felt how dearly this praise had been earned, and already almost repented of having deserved it. There was a sadness in [242] the countenance of Alethe, as I took leave of her, to which the forebodings of my own heart but too faithfully responded; nor could I help fearing, as her hand parted lingeringly from mine, that I had, by this sacrifice, placed her beyond my reach for ever.

Having lighted me a lamp, which, in these recesses, even at noon, is necessary, the holy man led me to the entrance of the grotto;—and here, I blush to say, my career of hypocrisy began. With the sole view of obtaining another glance at Alethe, I turned humbly to solicit the benediction of the Christian, and, having conveyed to her, as I bent reverently down, as much of the deep feeling of my soul as looks could express, with a desponding spirit I hurried into the cavern.

A short passage led me to the chamber within,—the walls of which I found covered, like those of the grottos of Lycopolis, with paintings, which, though executed long ages ago, looked fresh as if their colours were but laid on yesterday. They were, all of them, representations of rural and domestic scenes; and, in [243] the greater number, the melancholy imagination of the artist had called Death in, as usual, to throw his shadow over the picture.

My attention was particularly drawn to one series of subjects, throughout the whole of which the same group—a youth, a maiden, and two aged persons, who appeared to be the father and mother of the girl,—were represented in all the details of their daily life. The looks and attitudes of the young people denoted that they were lovers; and, sometimes, they were seen sitting under a canopy of flowers, with their eyes fixed on each other's faces, as though they could never look away; sometimes, they appeared walking along the banks of the Nile,

> ———on one of those sweet nights
> When Isis, the pure star of lovers, lights
> Her bridal crescent o'er the holy stream,—
> When wandering youths and maidens watch her beam,
> And number o'er the nights she hath to run,
> Ere she again embrace her bridegroom sun.

[244]

Through all these scenes of endearment the two elder persons stood by;—their calm countenances touched with a share of that bliss, in whose perfect light the young lovers were basking. Thus far, all was happiness,—but the sad lesson of mortality was to come. In the last picture of the series, one of the figures was missing. It was that of the young maiden, who had disappeared from among them. On the brink of a dark lake stood the three who remained; while a boat, just departing for the City of the Dead, told too plainly the end of their dream of happiness.

This memorial of a sorrow of other times—of a sorrow, ancient as death itself,—was not wanting to deepen the melancholy of my mind, or to add to the weight of the many bodings that pressed on it.

After a night, as it seemed, of anxious and unsleeping thought, I rose from my bed and returned to the garden. I found the Christian alone,—seated, under the shade of one of his trees, at a small table, with a volume unrolled before him, while a beautiful antelope lay sleeping at his feet. Struck forcibly by the contrast which he presented to those haughty priests, whom I had seen surrounded by the pomp and gorgeousness of temples, "Is this, then," thought I, "the faith, before which the world trembles—its temple the desert, its treasury a book, and its High Priest the solitary dweller of the rock!"

[245]

He had prepared for me a simple, but hospitable, repast, of which fruits from his own garden, the white bread of Olyra, and the juice of the honey-cane were the most costly luxuries. His manner to me was even more cordial than before; but the absence of Alethe, and, still more, the ominous reserve, with which he not only, himself, refrained from all mention of her name, but eluded the few inquiries, by which I sought to lead to it, seemed to confirm all the fears I had felt in parting from her.

[246]

She had acquainted him, it was evident, with the whole history of our flight. My reputation as a philosopher—my desire to become a Christian—all was already known to the zealous Anchoret, and the subject of my conversion was the very first on which he entered. O pride of philosophy, how wert thou then humbled, and with what shame did I stand, casting down my eyes, before that venerable man, as, with ingenuous trust in the sincerity of my intention, he welcomed me to a participation of his holy hope, and imprinted the Kiss of Charity on my infidel brow!

Embarrassed as I felt by the consciousness of hypocrisy, I was even still more perplexed by my total ignorance of the real tenets of the faith to which I professed myself a convert. Abashed and confused, and with a heart sick at its own deceit, I heard the animated and eloquent gratulations of the Christian, as though they were words in a dream, without link or meaning; nor could disguise but by the mockery of a reverential bow, at every pause, [247] the entire want of self-possession, and even of speech, under which I laboured.

A few minutes more of such trial, and I must have avowed my imposture. But the holy man saw my embarrassment;—and, whether mistaking it for awe, or knowing it to be ignorance, relieved me from my perplexity by, at once, changing the theme. Having gently awakened his antelope from its sleep, "You have heard," he said, "I doubt not, of my brother-anchoret, Paul, who, from his cave in the marble mountains, near the Red Sea, sends hourly 'the sacrifice of thanksgiving' to heaven. Of *his* walks, they tell me, a lion is the companion; but, for me," he added, with a playful and significant smile, "who try my powers of taming but on the gentler animals, this feeble child of the desert is a far fitter play-mate." Then, taking his staff, and putting the time-worn volume which he had been reading into a large goat-skin pouch, [248] that hung by his side, "I will now," said he, "lead thee over my rocky kingdom,—that thou mayst see in what drear and barren places, that 'fruit of the spirit,' Peace, may be gathered."

To speak of peace to a heart like mine, at that moment, was like talking of some distant harbour to the mariner sinking at sea. In vain did I look round for some sign of Alethe;—in vain make an effort even to utter her name. Consciousness of my own deceit, as well as a fear of awakening in Melanius any suspicion that might frustrate my only hope, threw a fetter over my spirit and checked my tongue. In silence, therefore, I followed, while the cheerful old man, with slow, but firm, step, ascended the rock, by the same ladders which I had mounted on the preceding night.

[249]

During the time when the Decian Persecution was raging, many Christians of this neighbourhood, he informed me, had taken refuge under his protection, in these grottos; and the chapel on the summit, where I had found them at prayer, was, in those times of danger, their place of retreat, where, by drawing up these ladders, they were enabled to secure themselves from pursuit.

From the top of the rock, the view, on either side, embraced the two extremes of fertility and desolation; nor could the Epicurean and the Anchoret, who now gazed from that height, be at any loss to indulge their respective tastes, between the living luxuriance of the world on one side, and the dead repose of the desert on the other. When we turned to the river, what a picture of animation presented itself! Near us, to the south, were the graceful colonnades of Antinoë, its proud, populous streets, and triumphal monuments. On the opposite shore, rich plains, teeming with cultivation to the water's edge, offered up, as from verdant altars, their fruits to the sun; while, beneath us, the Nile,

[250]

——the glorious stream,
That late between its banks was seen to glide,—
With shrines and marble cities, on each side,
Glittering, like jewels strung along a chain,—
Had now sent forth its waters, and o'er plain
And valley, like a giant from his bed
Rising with outstretch'd limbs, superbly spread.

From this scene, on one side of the mountain, we had but to turn round our eyes, and it was as if nature herself had become suddenly extinct;—a wide waste of sands, bleak and interminable, wearying out the sun with its sameness of desolation;—black, burnt-up rocks, that stood as barriers, at which life stopped;—while the only signs of animation, past or present, were the foot-prints, here and there, of an antelope or ostrich, or the bones of dead camels, as they lay whitening at a distance, marking out the track of the caravans over the waste. [251]

After listening, while he contrasted, in a few eloquent words, the two regions of life and death on whose confines we stood, I again descended with my guide to the garden we had left. From thence, turning into a path along the mountain-side, he conducted me to another row of grottos, facing the desert, which had once, he said, been the abode of those brethren in Christ, who had fled with him to this solitude from the crowded world,—but which death had, within a few months, rendered tenantless. A cross of red stone, and a few faded trees, were the only traces these solitaries had left behind.

A silence of some minutes succeeded, while we descended to the edge of the canal; and I saw opposite, among the rocks, that solitary cave, which had so chilled me with its aspect on the preceding night. By the bank we found one of those rustic boats, which the Egyptians construct of planks of wild thorn, bound rudely together with bands of papyrus. Placing ourselves [252] in this boat, and rather impelling than rowing it across, we made our way through the foul and shallow flood, and landed directly under the site of the cave.

This dwelling, as I have already mentioned, was situated upon a ledge of the rock; and, being provided with a sort of window or aperture to admit the light of heaven, was accounted, I found, more cheerful than the grottos on the other side of the ravine. But there was a dreariness in the whole region around, to which light only lent more horror. The dead whiteness of the rocks, as they stood, like ghosts, in the sunshine;—that melancholy pool, half lost in the sands;—all gave me the idea of a wasting world. To dwell in such a place seemed to me like a living death; and when the Christian, as we entered the cave, said, "Here is to be thy home," prepared as I was for the worst, my resolution gave way;—every feeling of disappointed passion and humbled pride, [253] which had been gathering round my heart for the last few hours, found a vent at once, and I burst into tears!

Well accustomed to human weakness, and perhaps guessing at some of the sources of mine, the good Hermit, without appearing to notice this emotion, expatiated, with a cheerful air, on, what he called, the many comforts of my dwelling. Sheltered, he said, from the dry, burning wind of the south, my porch would inhale the fresh breeze of the Dog-star. Fruits from his own mountain-garden should furnish my repast. The well of the neighbouring rock would supply my beverage; and, "here," he continued,—lowering his voice into a more solemn tone, as he placed upon the table the volume which he had brought,—"here, my son, is that 'well of living waters,' in which alone thou wilt find lasting refreshment or peace!" Thus saying, he descended the rock to his boat, and after a few plashes of his oar had died upon my ear, the solitude and silence around me was complete.

[254]

CHAP. XVII.

What a fate was mine!—but a few weeks since, presiding over that splendid Festival of the Garden, with all the luxuries of existence tributary in my train; and now,—self-humbled into a solitary outcast,—the hypocritical pupil of a Christian anchoret,—without even the excuse of fanaticism, or of any other madness, but that of love, wild love, to extenuate my fall! Were there a hope that, by this humiliating waste of existence, I might purchase but a glimpse, now and then, of Alethe, even the depths of the desert, with such a chance, would be welcome. But to live—and live thus—*without* her, was a misery which I neither foresaw nor could endure.

Hating even to look upon the den to which I was doomed, I hurried out into the air, and found my way, along the rocks, to [256] the desert. The sun was going down, with that blood-red hue, which he so frequently wears, in this clime, at his setting. I saw the sands, stretching out, like a sea, to the horizon, as if their waste extended to the very verge of the world,—and, in the bitterness of my feelings, rejoiced to see so much of creation rescued, even by this barren liberty, from the grasp of man. The thought seemed to relieve my wounded pride, and, as I wandered over the dim and boundless solitude, to be thus free, even amid blight and desolation, appeared a blessing.

The only living thing I saw was a restless swallow, whose wings were of the hue of the grey sands over which he fluttered. "Why may not the mind, like this bird, take the colour of the desert, and sympathise in its austerity, its freedom, and its calm?"—thus, between despondence and defiance, did I ask myself, endeavouring to face with fortitude what yet my heart sickened to contemplate. But the effort was unavailing. Overcome by that vast solitude, whose repose was not the slumber of peace, but the sullen and burning silence of hate, I felt my spirit give way, and even love itself yield to despair.

[257]

Seating myself on a fragment of a rock, and covering my eyes with my hands, I made an effort to shut out the overwhelming prospect. But in vain—it was still before me, deepened by all that fancy could add; and when, again looking up, I saw the last red ray of the sun, shooting across that melancholy and lifeless waste, it seemed to me like the light of the comet that once desolated this world, shining out luridly over the ruin that it had made!

Appalled by my own gloomy imaginations, I turned towards the ravine; and, notwithstanding the disgust with which I had left my dwelling, was not ill pleased to find my way, over the rocks, to it again. On approaching the cave, to my astonishment, I saw a light within. At such a moment, any vestige of life was welcome, and I hailed the unexpected appearance with pleasure. On entering, however, I found the chamber as lonely as I had left it. The light came from a lamp that burned brightly on the table; beside it was unfolded the volume which Melanius had brought, and upon the leaves—oh, joy and surprise—lay the well-known cross of Alethe!

[258]

What hand, but her own, could have prepared this reception for me?—The very thought sent a hope into my heart, before which all despondency fled. Even the gloom of the desert was forgotten, and my cave at once brightened into a bower. She had here reminded me, herself, by this sacred memorial, of the vow which I had pledged to her under the Hermit's rock; and I now scrupled not to reiterate the same daring promise, though conscious that through hypocrisy alone I could fulfil it.

[259]

Eager to prepare myself for my task of imposture, I sat down to the volume, which I now found to be the Hebrew Scriptures; and the first sentence, on which my eyes fell, was—"The Lord hath commanded the blessing, even Life for evermore!" Startled by these words, in which the Spirit of my dream seemed again to pronounce his assuring prediction, I raised my eyes from the page, and repeated the sentence over and over, as if to try whether the sounds had any charm or spell, to reawaken that faded illusion in my soul. But, no—the rank frauds of the Memphian priesthood had dispelled all my trust in the promises of religion. My heart had again relapsed into its gloom of scepticism, and, to the word of "Life," the only answer it sent back was, "Death!"

Impatient, however, to possess myself of the elements of a faith, on which,—whatever it might promise for hereafter,—I felt that my happiness here depended, I turned over the pages with an earnestness and avidity, such as never even the most [260] favourite of my studies had awakened in me. Though, like all, who seek but the surface of learning, I flew desultorily over the leaves, lighting only on the more prominent and shining points, I yet found myself, even in this undisciplined career, arrested, at every page, by the awful, the supernatural sublimity, the alternate melancholy and grandeur of the images that crowded upon me.

I had, till now, known the Hebrew theology but through the platonising refinements of Philo;—as, in like manner, for my knowledge of the Christian doctrine I was indebted to my brother Epicureans, Lucian and Celsus. Little, therefore, was I prepared for the simple majesty, the high tone of inspiration,—the poetry, in short, of heaven that breathed throughout these oracles. Could admiration have kindled faith, I should, that night, have been a believer; so elevated, so awed was my imagination by that [261] wonderful book,—its warnings of woe, its announcements of glory, and its unrivalled strains of adoration and sorrow.

Hour after hour, with the same eager and desultory curiosity, did I turn over the leaves;—and when, at length, I lay down to rest, my fancy was still haunted by the impressions it had received. I went again through the various scenes of which I had read; again called up, in sleep, the bright images that had charmed me, and, when wakened at day-break by the Hymn from the chapel, fancied myself still listening to the sound of the winds, sighing mournfully through the harps of Israel on the willows.

Starting from my bed, I hurried out upon the rock, with a hope that, among the tones of that morning choir, I might be able to distinguish the sweet voice of Alethe. But the strain had ceased;—I caught only the last notes of the Hymn, as, echoing up that lonely valley, they died away into the silence of the desert.

[262]

With the first glimpse of light I was again at my study, and, notwithstanding the distraction both of my thoughts and looks towards the half-seen grottos of the Anchoret, pursued it perseveringly through the day. Still alive, however, but to the eloquence, the poetry of what I read, of its connection or authenticity, as a history, I never paused to consider. My fancy being alone interested by it, to fancy I referred all it contained; and, passing rapidly from annals to prophecy, from narration to song, regarded the whole but as a tissue of splendid allegories, in which the melancholy of Egyptian associations was interwoven with the rich imagery of the East.

Towards sunset I saw the boat of Melanius on its way, across the canal, to my cave. Though he had no other companion than his graceful antelope, that stood snuffing the wild air of the desert, as if scenting its home, I felt his visit, even thus, to be a most welcome relief. It was the hour, he said, of his evening ramble up the mountain,—of his accustomed visit to those cisterns of the rock, from which he nightly drew his most precious beverage. While he spoke, I observed in his hand one of those earthen cups, in which the inhabitants of the wilderness are accustomed to collect the fresh dew among the rocks. Having proposed that I should accompany him in his walk, he led me, in the direction of the desert, up the side of the mountain that

[263]

rose above my dwelling, and which formed the southern wall or screen of the defile.

Near the summit we found a seat, where the old man paused to rest. It commanded a full view over the desert, and was by the side of one of those hollows in the rock, those natural reservoirs, in which the dews of night are treasured up for the refreshment of the dwellers in the wilderness. Having learned from me how far I had proceeded in my study, "In that light," said he, pointing to a small cloud in the east, which had been formed on the [264] horizon by the haze of the desert, and was now faintly reflecting the splendours of sunset,—"in that light stands Mount Sinai, of whose glory thou hast read; on whose summit was the scene of one of those awful revelations, in which the Almighty has, from time to time, renewed his communication with Man, and kept alive the remembrance of his own Providence in this world."

After a pause, as if absorbed in the immensity of the subject, the holy man continued his sublime theme. Looking back to the earliest annals of time, he showed how constantly every relapse of the human race into idolatry has been followed by some man-ifestation of divine power, chastening the proud by punishment, and winning back the humble by love. It was to preserve, he said, unextinguished upon earth, that vital truth,—the Creation of the world by one Supreme Being,—that God chose, from among the nations, an humble and enslaved race;—that he brought them [265] out of their captivity "on eagles' wings," and, surrounding every step of their course with miracles, placed them before the eyes of all succeeding generations, as the depositaries of his will, and the ever-during memorials of his power.

Passing, then, in review the long train of inspired interpreters, whose pens and whose tongues were made the echoes of the Di-vine voice, he traced[8], through the events of successive ages, the gradual unfolding of the dark scheme of Providence—darkness

---

[8] In the original the discourses of the Hermit are given much more at length.

without, but all light and glory within. The glimpses of a coming redemption, visible even through the wrath of heaven;—the long series of prophecy, through which this hope runs, burning and alive, like a spark through a chain;—the merciful preparation of the hearts of mankind for the great trial of their faith and obedience that was at hand, not only by miracles that appealed to the living, but by predictions launched into futurity to carry conviction to the yet unborn;—"through all these glorious and beneficent gradations we may track," said he, "the manifest footsteps of a Creator, advancing to his grand, ultimate end, the salvation of his creatures."

After some hours devoted to these holy instructions, we returned to the ravine, and Melanius left me at my cave; praying, as he parted from me,—with a benevolence I but ill, alas! deserved,—that my soul, under these lessons, might be "as a watered garden," and, ere long, bear "fruit unto life eternal."

Next morning, I was again at my study, and even more eager in the task than before. With the commentary of the Hermit freshly in my memory, I again read through, with attention, the Book of the Law. But in vain did I seek the promise of immortality in its pages. "It tells me," said I, "of a God coming down to earth, but of the ascent of Man to heaven it speaks not. The rewards, the punishments it announces, lie all on this side of the grave; nor did even the Omnipotent offer to his own chosen servants a hope beyond the impassable limits of this world. Where, then, is the salvation of which the Christian spoke? or, if Death be at the root of the faith, can Life spring out of it!"

Again, in the bitterness of disappointment, did I mock at my own willing self-delusion,—again rail at the arts of that traitress, Fancy, ever ready, like the Delilah of this book, to steal upon the slumbers of Reason, and deliver him up, shorn and powerless, to his foes. If deception—thought I, with a sigh—be necessary, at least let me not practise it on myself;—in the desperate alternative before me, let me rather be even hypocrite than dupe.

[266]

[267]

These self-accusing reflections, cheerless as they rendered [268] my task, did not abate, for a single moment, my industry in pursuing it. I read on and on, with a sort of sullen apathy, neither charmed by style, nor transported by imagery,—that fatal blight in my heart having communicated itself to my fancy and taste. The curses and the blessings, the glory and the ruin, which the historian recorded and the prophet predicted, seemed all of this world,—all, temporal and earthly. That mortality, of which the fountain-head had tasted, tinged the whole stream; and when I read the words, "all are of the dust, and all turn to dust again," a feeling, like the wind of the desert, came witheringly over me. Love, Beauty, Glory, every thing most bright upon earth, appeared sinking before my eyes, under this dreadful doom, into one general mass of corruption and silence.

Possessed by the image of desolation I had called up, I laid my head on the book, in a paroxysm of despair. Death, in all his [269] most ghastly varieties, passed before me; and I had continued thus for some time, as under the influence of a fearful vision, when the touch of a hand upon my shoulder roused me. Looking up, I saw the Anchoret standing by my side;—his countenance beaming with that sublime tranquillity, which a hope, beyond this earth, alone can bestow. How I envied him!

We again took our way to the seat upon the mountain,—the gloom in my own mind making every thing around me more gloomy. Forgetting my hypocrisy in my feelings, I, at once, avowed to him all the doubts and fears which my study of the morning had awakened.

"Thou art yet, my son," he answered, "but on the threshold of our faith. Thou hast seen but the first rudiments of the Divine plan;—its full and consummate perfection hath not yet opened upon thee. However glorious that manifestation of Divinity on Mount Sinai, it was but the forerunner of another, still more [270] glorious, that, in the fulness of time, was to burst upon the world; when all, that had seemed dim and incomplete, was to be perfected, and the promises, shadowed out by the 'spirit of prophecy,' realized;—when the silence, that lay, as a seal, on the future, was to be broken, and the glad tidings of life and immortality proclaimed to the world!"

Observing my features brighten at these words, the pious man continued. Anticipating some of the holy knowledge that was in store for me, he traced, through all its wonders and mercies, the great work of Redemption, dwelling on every miraculous circumstance connected with it;—the exalted nature of the Being, by whose ministry it was accomplished, the noblest and first created of the Sons of God, inferior only to the one, self-existent Father;—the mysterious incarnation of this heavenly messenger;—the miracles that authenticated his divine mission;—the example of obedience to God and love to man, which he set, as a shining light, before the world for ever;—and, lastly and chiefly, his death and resurrection, by which the covenant of mercy was sealed, and "life and immortality brought to light."

"Such," continued the Hermit, "was the Mediator, promised through all time, to 'make reconciliation for iniquity,' to change death into life, and bring 'healing on his wings' to a darkened world. Such was the last crowning dispensation of that God of benevolence, in whose hands sin and death are but instruments of everlasting good, and who, through apparent evil and temporary retribution, bringing all things 'out of darkness into his marvellous light,' proceeds watchfully and unchangingly to the great, final object of his providence,—the restoration of the whole human race to purity and happiness!"

With a mind astonished, if not touched, by these discourses, I returned to my cave; and found the lamp, as before, ready lighted to receive me. The volume which I had been reading was replaced by another, which lay open upon the table, with a branch of fresh palm between its leaves. Though I could not have a doubt to whose gentle hand I was indebted for this invisible superintendence over my studies, there was yet a something in it,

[271]

[272]

so like spiritual interposition, that it awed me;—and never more than at this moment, when, on approaching the volume, I saw, as the light glistened over its silver letters, that it was the very Book of Life of which the Hermit had spoken!

The orison of the Christians had sounded through the valley, before I raised my eyes from that sacred volume; and the second hour of the sun found me again over its pages.

CHAP. XVIII.

In this mode of existence did I pass some days;—my mornings devoted to reading, my nights to listening, under the canopy of heaven, to the holy eloquence of Melanius. The perseverance with which I enquired, and the quickness with which I learned, soon succeeded in deceiving my benevolent instructor, who mistook curiosity for zeal and knowledge for belief. Alas! cold, and barren, and earthly was that knowledge,—the word, without the spirit, the shape, without the life. Even when, as a relief from hypocrisy, I persuaded myself that I believed, it was but a brief delusion, a faith, whose hope crumbled at the touch,—like the fruit of the desert-shrub, shining and empty!

But, though my soul was still dark, the good Hermit saw not into its depths. The very facility of my belief, which might have suggested some doubt of its sincerity, was but regarded by his innocent zeal, as a more signal triumph of the truth. His own ingenuousness led him to a ready trust in others; and the examples of such conversion as that of the philosopher, Justin, who received the light into his soul during a walk by the sea-shore, had prepared him for illuminations of the spirit, even more rapid than mine.

During this time, I neither saw nor heard of Alethe;—nor could my patience have endured so long a privation, had not those mute vestiges of her presence, that welcomed me every night on my return, made me feel that I was still living under her gentle influence, and that her sympathy hung round every step of my progress. Once, too, when I ventured to speak her name to Melanius, though he answered not my enquiry, there was a smile, I thought, of promise upon his countenance, which love, [275] more alive than faith, interpreted as it wished.

At length,—it was on the sixth or seventh evening of my solitude, when I lay resting at the door of my cave, alter the study of the day,—I was startled by hearing my name called loudly from the opposite rocks, and looking up, saw, on the cliff near the deserted grottos, Melanius and—oh, I could not doubt—my Alethe by his side!

Though I had never ceased, since the first night of my return from the desert, to flatter myself with the fancy that I was still living in her presence, the actual sight of her again made me feel what an age we had been separated. She was clothed all in white, and, as she stood in the last remains of the sunshine, appeared to my too prophetic fancy like a parting spirit, whose last footsteps on earth that glory encircled.

With a delight only to be imagined, I saw them descend the rocks, and placing themselves in the boat, proceed towards my [276] cave. To disguise from Melanius the feelings with which we met was impossible;—nor did Alethe even attempt to make a secret of her innocent joy. Though blushing at her own happiness, she could as little conceal it, as the clear waters of Ethiopia can hide their gold. Every look, too, every word, spoke a fulness of affection, to which, doubtful as I was of our tenure of happiness, I knew not how to answer.

I was not long, however, left ignorant of the bright fate that awaited me; but, as we wandered or rested among the rocks, learned every thing that had been arranged since our parting. She had made the Hermit, I found, acquainted with all that had passed between us; had told him, without reserve, every incident of our voyage,—the avowals, the demonstrations of affection on one side, and the deep sentiment that gratitude had awakened on the other. Too wise to regard feelings, so natural, with [277] severity,—knowing that they were of heaven, and but made evil by man,—the good Hermit had heard of our attachment with pleasure; and, proved as he thought the purity of my views had been, by the fidelity with which I had delivered up my trust into his hands, saw, in my affection for the young orphan, but a providential resource against that friendless solitude in which his death must soon leave her.

As I collected these particulars from their discourse, I could hardly trust my ears. It seemed too much happiness to be real; nor can words give an idea of the joy—the shame—the wonder with which I listened, while the holy man himself declared, that he awaited but the moment, when he should find me worthy of becoming a member of the Christian Church, to give me also the hand of Alethe in that sacred union, which alone sanctifies love, and makes the faith, which it pledges, heavenly. It was but yesterday, he added, that his young charge, herself, after a preparation of prayer and repentance, such as even her pure spirit required, had been admitted, by the sacred ordinance of baptism, into the bosom of the faith;—and the white garment she wore, and the ring of gold on her finger, "were symbols," he said, "of that New Life into which she had been initiated."

[278]

I raised my eyes to her as he spoke, but withdrew them again, dazzled and confused. Even her beauty, to my imagination, seemed to have undergone some brightening change; and the contrast between that open and happy countenance, and the un-blest brow of the infidel that stood before her, abashed me into a sense of unworthiness, and almost checked my rapture.

To that night, however, I look back, as an epoch in my exis-tence. It proved that sorrow is not the only awakener of devotion, but that joy may sometimes call the holy spark into life. Re-turning to my cave, with a heart full, even to oppression, of its happiness, I knew no other relief to my overcharged feelings than that of throwing myself on my knees, and, for the first time in my life, uttering a prayer, that if, indeed, there were a Being who watched over mankind, he would send down one ray of his truth

[279]

into my soul, and make it worthy of the blessings, both here and hereafter, proffered to me!

My days now rolled on in a perfect dream of happiness. Every hour of the morning was welcomed as bringing nearer and nearer the blest time of sunset, when the Hermit and Alethe never failed to pay their visit to my now charmed cave, where her smile left a light, at each parting, that lasted till her return. Then, our rambles, by star-light, over the mountain;—our pauses, on the way, to contemplate the bright wonders of that heaven above us;—our repose by the cistern of the rock, and our silent listening, through hours that seemed minutes, to the holy eloquence of our [280] teacher;—all, all was happiness of the most heartfelt kind, and such as even the doubts, the cold, lingering doubts, that still hung, like a mist, around my heart, could neither cloud nor chill.

When the moonlight nights returned, we used to venture into the desert; and those sands, which but lately had appeared to me so desolate, now wore even a cheerful and smiling aspect. To the light, innocent heart of Alethe every thing was a source of enjoyment. For her, even the desert had its jewels and flowers; and, sometimes, her delight was to search among the sands for those beautiful pebbles of jasper that abound in them;—sometimes, her eyes sparkled on finding, perhaps, a stunted marigold, or one of those bitter, scarlet flowers, that lend their mockery of ornament to the desert. In all these pursuits and pleasures the good Hermit took a share,—mingling with them occasionally the reflections of a benevolent piety, that lent its own cheerful hue [281] to all the works of creation, and saw the consoling truth "God is Love," written legibly every where.

Such was, for a few weeks, my blissful life. Oh mornings of hope, oh nights of happiness, with what mournful pleasure do I retrace your flight, and how reluctantly pass to the sad events that followed!

During this time, in compliance with the wishes of Melanius, who seemed unwilling that I should become wholly estranged from the world, I occasionally paid a visit to the neighbouring city, Antinoë, which, as the capital of the Thebaid, is the centre of all the luxury of Upper Egypt. Here,—so changed was my every feeling by the all-transforming passion that possessed me,—I wandered, unamused and uninterested by either the scenes or the people that surrounded me, and, sighing for that rocky solitude where Alethe breathed, felt *this* to be the wilderness, and *that*, the world.

Even the thoughts of my own native Athens, that were called up, at every step, by the light, Grecian architecture of this imperial city, did not awaken one single regret in my heart—one wish to exchange even an hour of my desert for the best luxuries and honours that awaited me in the Garden. I saw the arches of triumph;—I walked under the superb portico, which encircles the whole city with its marble shade;—I stood in the Circus of the Sun, by whose rose-coloured pillars the mysterious movements of the Nile are measured;—all these bright ornaments of glory and art, as well as the gay multitude that enlivened them, I saw with an unheeding eye. If they awakened in me any thought, it was the mournful idea, that, one day, like Thebes and Heliopolis, this pageant would pass away, leaving nothing behind but a few mouldering ruins,—like the sea-shells found where the ocean has been,—to tell that the great tide of Life was once there!

But, though indifferent thus to all that had formerly attracted me, there were subjects, once alien to my heart, on which it was now most tremblingly alive; and some rumours which had reached me, in one of my visits to the city, of an expected change in the policy of the Emperor towards the Christians, filled me with apprehensions as new as they were dreadful to me.

The peace and even favour which the Christians enjoyed, during the first four years of the reign of Valerian, had removed from them all fear of a renewal of those horrors, which they had experienced under the rule of his predecessor, Decius. Of late, however, some less friendly dispositions had manifested themselves. The bigots of the court, taking alarm at the spread of the new faith, had succeeded in filling the mind of the monarch with that religious jealousy, which is the ever-ready parent of cruelty and injustice. Among these counsellors of evil was Macrianus, the Prætorian Prefect, who was, by birth, an Egyptian, and—so akin is superstition to intolerance—had long made himself no- [284] torious by his addiction to the dark practices of demon-worship and magic.

From this minister, who was now high in the favour of Va-lerian, the expected measures of severity against the Christians, it was supposed, would emanate. All tongues, in all quarters, were busy with the news. In the streets, in the public gardens, on the steps of the temples, I saw, every where, groups of enquirers collected, and heard the name of Macrianus upon every tongue. It was dreadful, too, to observe, in the countenances of those who spoke, the variety of feeling with which the rumour was discussed, according as they desired or dreaded its truth,—ac-cording as they were likely to be among the torturers or the victims.

Alarmed, though still ignorant of the whole extent of the dan-ger, I hurried back to the ravine, and, going at once to the grotto of Melanius, detailed to him every particular of the intelligence I had collected. He heard me with a composure, which I mistook, [285] alas, for confidence in his security; and, naming the hour for our evening walk, retired into his grotto.

At the accustomed time Alethe and he were at my cave. It was evident that he had not communicated to her the intelligence which I had brought, for never did brow wear such a happiness as that which now played round hers;—it was, alas, *not* of this earth! Melanius, himself, though composed, was thoughtful; and the solemnity, almost approaching to melancholy, with which he placed the hand of Alethe in mine—in the performance, too, of a ceremony that *ought* to have filled my heart with joy—saddened and alarmed me. This ceremony was our betrothment,—the

plighting of our faith to each other,—which we now solemnized
on the rock before the door of my cave, in the face of that sunset
heaven, with its one star standing as witness. After a blessing
from the Hermit on our spousal pledge, I placed the ring,—the
earnest of our future union—on her finger, and, in the blush,
with which she surrendered her whole heart to me at that instant,
forgot every thing but my happiness, and felt secure, even against
fate!

We took our accustomed walk over the rocks and on the
desert. The moon was so bright,—like the daylight, indeed, of
other climes—that we could see plainly the tracks of the wild
antelopes in the sand; and it was not without a slight tremble of
feeling in his voice, as if some melancholy analogy occurred to
him as he spoke, that the good Hermit said, "I have observed
in my walks, that where-ever the track of that gentle animal is
seen, there is, almost always, the foot-print of a beast of prey
near it." He regained, however, his usual cheerfulness before we
parted, and fixed the following evening for an excursion, on the
other side of the ravine, to a point, looking, he said, "towards
that northern region of the desert, where the hosts of the Lord
encamped in their departure out of bondage."

Though, in the presence of Alethe, my fears, even for herself,
were forgotten in that perpetual element of happiness, which
encircled her like the air that she breathed, no sooner was I alone
than vague terrors and bodings crowded upon me. In vain did
I try to reason myself out of my fears by dwelling on the most
cheering circumstances,—the reverence with which Melanius
was regarded, even by the Pagans, and the inviolate security with
which he had lived through the most perilous periods, not only
safe himself, but affording sanctuary in his grottos to others.
When, somewhat calmed by these considerations, I sunk off to
sleep, dark, horrible dreams took possession of my mind. Scenes
of death and of torment passed confusedly before me, and, when
I awoke, it was with the fearful impression that all these horrors

[286]

[287]

were real.

CHAP. XIX.

At length, the day dawned,—that dreadful day. Impatient to be relieved from my suspense, I threw myself into my boat,—the same in which we had performed our happy voyage,—and, as fast as oars could speed me, hurried away to the city. I found the suburbs silent and solitary, but, as I approached the Forum, loud yells, like those of barbarians in combat, struck on my ear, and, when I entered it,—great God, what a spectacle presented itself! The imperial edict against the Christians had arrived during the night, and already the wild fury of bigotry was let loose.

Under a canopy, in the middle of the Forum, was the tribunal of the Governor. Two statues, one of Apollo, the other of Osiris, stood at the bottom of the steps that led up to his judgment-seat.

Before these idols were shrines, to which the devoted Christians were dragged from all quarters by the soldiers and mob, and there compelled to recant, by throwing incense into the flame, or, on their refusal, hurried away to torture and death. It was an appalling scene;—the consternation, the cries of some of the victims,—the pale, silent resolution of others;—the fierce shouts of laughter that broke from the multitude, when the frankincense, dropped on the altar, proclaimed some denier of Christ; and the fiend-like triumph with which the courageous Confessors, who avowed their faith, were led away to the flames;—never could I have conceived such an assemblage of horrors!

Though I gazed but for a few minutes, in those minutes I felt enough for years. Already did the form of Alethe flit before me through that tumult;—I heard them shout her name;—her shriek fell on my ear; and the very thought so palsied me with terror, that I stood fixed and statue-like on the spot.

Recollecting, however, the fearful preciousness of every moment, and that—perhaps, at this very instant—some emissaries of blood might be on their way to the grottos, I rushed wildly out of the Forum, and made my way to the quay.

The streets were now crowded; but I ran headlong through the multitude, and was already under the portico leading down to the river,—already saw the boat that was to bear me to Alethe,—when a Centurion stood sternly in my path, and I was surrounded and arrested by soldiers! It was in vain that I implored, that I struggled with them as for life, assuring them that I was a stranger,—that I was an Athenian,—that I was—*not* a Christian. The precipitation of my flight was sufficient evidence against me, and unrelentingly, and by force, they bore me away to the quarters of their Chief.   [291]

It was enough to drive me to madness! Two hours, two frightful hours, was I kept waiting the arrival of the Tribune of their Legion[9],—my brain burning with a thousand fears and imaginations, which every passing minute made more likely to be realised. Every thing, too, that I could collect from the conversations around me but added to the agonising apprehensions with which I was racked. Troops, it was said, had been sent in all directions through the neighbourhood, to bring in the rebellious Christians, and make them bow before the Gods of the Empire. With horror, too, I heard of Orcus,—Orcus, the High Priest of Memphis,—as one of the principal instigators of this sanguinary edict, and as here present in Antinoë, animating and directing its execution.

In this state of torture I remained till the arrival of the Tri-   [292]
bune. Absorbed in my own thoughts, I had not perceived his entrance;—till, hearing a voice, in a tone of friendly surprise,

---

[9] A rank, resembling that of Colonel.

exclaim, "Alciphron!" I looked up, and in this legionary Chief recognised a young Roman of rank, who had held a military command, the year before, at Athens, and was one of the most distinguished visitors of the Garden. It was no time, however, for courtesies;—he was proceeding with cordiality to greet me, but, having heard him order my instant release, I could wait for no more. Acknowledging his kindness but by a grasp of the hand, I flew off, like one frantic, through the streets, and, in a few minutes, was on the river.

My sole hope had been to reach the grottos before any of the detached parties should arrive, and, by a timely flight across the desert, rescue, at least, Alethe from their fury. The ill-fated delay that had occurred rendered this hope almost desperate; but the tranquillity I found every where as I proceeded down the river, and the fond confidence I still cherished in the sacredness of the Hermit's retreat, kept my heart from giving way altogether under its terrors.

Between the current and my oars, the boat flew, like wind, along the waters; and I was already near the rocks of the ravine, when I saw, turning out of the canal into the river, a barge crowded with people, and glittering with arms! How did I ever survive the shock of that sight? The oars dropped, as if struck out of my hands, into the water, and I sat, helplessly gazing, as that terrific vision approached. In a few minutes, the current brought us together;—and I saw, on the deck of the barge, Alethe and the Hermit surrounded by soldiers!

We were already passing each other when, with a desperate effort, I sprang from my boat and lighted upon the edge of their vessel. I knew not what I did, for despair was my only prompter. Snatching at the sword of one of the soldiers, as I stood tottering on the edge, I had succeeded in wresting it out of his hands, when, at the same moment, I received a thrust of a lance from one of his comrades, and fell backward into the river. I can just remember rising again and making a grasp at the side of the vessel;—but the shock, the faintness from my wound, deprived me of all consciousness, and a shriek from Alethe, as I sunk, is all I can recollect of what followed.

Would I had then died!—Yet, no, Almighty Being,—I should have died in darkness, and I have lived to know Thee!

On returning to my senses, I found myself reclined on a couch, in a splendid apartment, the whole appearance of which being Grecian, I, for a moment, forgot all that had passed, and imagined myself in my own home at Athens. But too soon the whole dreadful certainty flashed upon me; and, starting wildly—disabled as [295] I was—from my couch, I called loudly, and with the shriek of a maniac, on Alethe.

I was in the house, I found, of my friend and disciple, the young Tribune, who had made the Governor acquainted with my name and condition, and had received me under his roof, when brought, bleeding and insensible, to Antinoë. From him I now learned at once,—for I could not wait for details,—the sum of all that had happened in that dreadful interval. Melanius was no more,—Alethe, still alive, but in prison!

"Take me to her"—I had but time to say—"take me to her instantly, and let me die by her side,"—when, nature again failing under such shocks, I relapsed into insensibility. In this state I continued for near an hour, and, on recovering, found the Tribune by my side. The horrors, he said, of the Forum were, for that day, over,—but what the morrow might bring, he shuddered to contemplate. His nature, it was plain, revolted from the inhuman [296] duties in which he was engaged. Touched by the agonies he saw me suffer, he, in some degree, relieved them, by promising that I should, at night-fall, be conveyed to the prison, and, if possible, through his influence, gain access to Alethe. She might yet, he added, be saved, could I succeed in persuading her to comply with the terms of the edict, and make sacrifice to the Gods.—"Otherwise," said he, "there is no hope;—the vindictive Orcus, who has resisted even this short respite of mercy, will, to-morrow, inexorably demand his prey."

He then related to me, at my own request,—though every word was torture,—all the harrowing details of the proceeding before the Tribunal. "I have seen courage," said he, "in its noblest forms, in the field; but the calm intrepidity with which that aged Hermit endured torments—which it was hardly less torment to witness—surpassed all that I could have conceived of human fortitude!"

My poor Alethe, too,—in describing to me her conduct, the brave man wept like a child. Overwhelmed, he said, at first by her apprehensions for my safety, she had given way to a full burst of womanly weakness. But no sooner was she brought before the Tribunal, and the declaration of her faith was demanded of her, than a spirit almost supernatural seemed to animate her whole form. "She raised her eyes," said he, "calmly, but with fervour, to heaven, while a blush was the only sign of mortal feeling on her features;—and the clear, sweet, and untrembling voice, with which she pronounced her dooming words, 'I am a Christian!' sent a thrill of admiration and pity throughout the multitude. Her youth, her loveliness, affected all hearts, and a cry of 'Save the young maiden!' was heard in all directions."

The implacable Orcus, however, would not hear of mercy. Resenting, as it appeared, with all his deadliest rancour, not only her own escape from his toils, but the aid with which, so fatally to his views, she had assisted mine, he demanded loudly, and in the name of the insulted sanctuary of Isis, her instant death. It was but by the firm intervention of the Governor, who shared the general sympathy in her fate, that the delay of another day was accorded, to give a chance to the young maiden of yet recalling her confession, and thus affording some pretext for saving her.

Even in yielding reluctantly to this brief respite, the inhuman Priest would accompany it with some mark of his vengeance. Whether for the pleasure (observed the Tribune) of mingling mockery with his cruelty, or as a warning to her of the doom she

[297]

[298]

must ultimately expect, he gave orders that there should be tied
round her brow one of those chaplets of coral[10], with which it is   [299]
the custom of young Christian maidens to array themselves on
the day of their martyrdom;—"and, thus fearfully adorned," said
he, "she was led away, amid the gaze of the pitying multitude, to
prison."

With these details the short interval till night-fall,—every
minute of which seemed an age,—was occupied. As soon as it
grew dark, I was placed upon a litter,—my wound, though not
dangerous, requiring such a conveyance,—and conducted, under
the guidance of my friend, to the prison. Through his interest
with the guard, we were without difficulty admitted, and I was
borne into the chamber where the maiden lay immured. Even the
veteran guardian of the place seemed touched with compassion
for his prisoner, and supposing her to be asleep, had the litter
placed gently near her.   [300]

She was half reclining, with her face hid in her hands, upon a
couch,—at the foot of which stood an idol, over whose hideous
features a lamp of naptha, hanging from the ceiling, shed a wild
and ghastly glare. On a table before the image stood a censer,
with a small vessel of incense beside it,—one grain of which,
thrown voluntarily into the flame, would, even now, save that
precious life. So strange, so fearful was the whole scene, that I
almost doubted its reality. Alethe! my own, happy Alethe! *can*
it, I thought, be thou that I look upon?

She now, slowly and with difficulty, raised her head from the
couch; on observing which, the kind Tribune withdrew, and we
were left alone. There was a paleness, as of death, over her
features; and those eyes, which when last I saw them, were but
too bright, too happy for this world, looked dim and sunken.
In raising herself up, she put her hand, as if from pain, to her
forehead, whose marble hue but appeared more death-like from   [301]

---

[10] "Une de ces couronnes de grain de corail, dont les vierges martyres ornoient
leurs cheveaux en allant à la mort." *Les Martyrs.*

those red bands that lay so awfully across it.

After wandering vaguely for a minute, her eyes rested upon me,—and, with a shriek, half terror, half joy, she sprung from the couch, and sunk upon her knees by my side. She had believed me dead; and, even now, scarcely trusted her senses. "My husband! my love!" she exclaimed; "oh, if thou comest to call me from this world, behold I am ready!" In saying thus, she pointed wildly to that ominous wreath, and then dropped her head down upon my knee, as if an arrow had pierced it.

"Alethe!"—I cried, terrified to the very soul by that mysterious pang,—and the sound of my voice seemed to reanimate her;—she looked up, with a faint smile, in my face. Her thoughts, which had evidently been wandering, became collected; and in [302] her joy at my safety, her sorrow at my suffering, she forgot wholly the fate that impended over herself. Love, innocent love, alone occupied all her thoughts; and the tenderness with which she spoke,—oh, at any other moment, how I would have listened, have lingered upon, have blessed every word!

But the time flew fast—the dreadful morrow was approaching. Already I saw her writhing in the hands of the torturer,—the flames, the racks, the wheels were before my eyes! Half frantic with the fear that her resolution was fixed, I flung myself from the litter, in an agony of weeping, and supplicated her, by the love she bore me, by the happiness that awaited us, by her own merciful God, who was too good to require such a sacrifice,—by all that the most passionate anxiety could dictate, I implored that she would avert from us the doom that was coming, and—but for once—comply with the vain ceremony demanded of her.

Shrinking from me, as I spoke,—but with a look more of [303] sorrow than reproach,—"What, thou, too!" she said mournfully,—"thou, into whose spirit I had fondly hoped the same heavenly truth had descended as into my own! Oh, be not thou leagued with those who would tempt me to 'make shipwreck of my faith!' Thou, who couldst alone bind me to life, use not thy

power; but let me die, as He I serve hath commanded,—die for
the Truth. Remember the holy lessons we heard on those nights,
those happy nights, when both the Present and Future smiled
upon us,—when even the gift of eternal life came more welcome
to my soul, from the blessed conviction that thou wert to be a
sharer in it;—shall I forfeit now that divine privilege? shall I
deny the true God, whom we then learned to love?

"No, my own betrothed," she continued,—pointing to the
two rings on her finger,—"behold these pledges,—they are both
sacred. I should have been as true to thee as I am now to
heaven,—nor in that life to which I am hastening shall our love [304]
be forgotten. Should the baptism of fire, through which I shall
pass to-morrow, make me worthy to be heard before the Throne
of Grace, I will intercede for thy soul—I will pray that it may
yet share with mine that 'inheritance, immortal and undefiled,'
which Mercy offers, and that thou,—my dear mother,—and I—"

She here dropped her voice; the momentary animation, with
which devotion and affection had inspired her, vanished;—and
a darkness overspread all her features, a livid darkness,—like
the coming of death—that made me shudder through every limb.
Seizing my hand convulsively, and looking at me with a fearful
eagerness, as if anxious to hear some consoling assurance from
my own lips,—"Believe me," she continued, "not all the torments they are preparing for me,—not even this deep, burning
pain in my brow, which they will hardly equal,—could be half
so dreadful to me, as the thought that I leave thee—" [305]

Here, her voice again failed; her head sunk upon my arm,
and—merciful God, let me forget what I then felt,—I saw that
she was dying! Whether I uttered any cry, I know not;—but
the Tribune came rushing into the chamber, and, looking on the
maiden, said, with a face full of horror, "It is but too true!"

He then told me in a low voice, what he had just learned
from the guardian of the prison, that the band round the young
Christian's brow was—oh horrible cruelty!—a compound of the

most deadly poison,—the hellish invention of Orcus, to satiate his vengeance, and make the fate of his poor victim secure. My first movement was to untie that fatal wreath,—but it would not come away—it would not come away!

Roused by the pain, she again looked in my face; but, unable to speak, took hastily from her bosom the small silver cross which she had brought with her from my cave. Having prest it to her own lips, she held it anxiously to mine, and seeing me kiss the holy symbol with fervour, looked happy, and smiled. The agony of death seemed to have passed away;—there came suddenly over her features a heavenly light, some share of which I felt descending into my own soul, and, in a few minutes more, she expired in my arms.

[306]

———————————————

Here ends the Manuscript; but, on the outer cover there is, in the hand-writing of a much later period, the following Notice, extracted, as it appears, from some Egyptian martyrology:—

"Alciphron,—an Epicurean philosopher, converted to Christianity A. D. 257, by a young Egyptian maiden, who suffered martyrdom in that year. Immediately upon her death he betook himself to the desert, and lived a life, it is said, of much holiness and penitence. During the persecution under Dioclesian, his sufferings for the faith were most exemplary; and, being at length, at an advanced age, condemned to hard labour, for refusing to comply with an Imperial edict, he died at the brass mines of Palestine, A. D. 297.—

[307]

"As Alciphron held the opinions maintained since by Arius, his memory has not been spared by Athanasian writers, who, among other charges, accuse him of having been addicted to the superstitions of Egypt. For this calumny, however, there appears to be no better foundation than a circumstance, recorded by one of his brother monks, that there was found, after his death, a small metal mirror, like those used in the ceremonies of Isis, suspended round his neck."

[308]

NOTES.

Page 17.—For the importance attached to dreams by the ancients, see *Jortin*, Remarks on Ecclesiastical History, vol. 1. p. 90.

Page 22.—"*The Pillar of Pillars*"—more properly, perhaps, "the column of the pillars." v. *Abdallatif*, Relation de l'Egypte, and the notes of *M. de Sacy*. The great portico round this column (formerly designated Pompey's, but now known to have been erected in honour of Dioclesian) was still standing, M. de Sacy says, in the time of Saladin. v. *Lord Valentia's Travels*.

Page 23.—Ammianus thus speaks of the state of Alexandria in his time, which was, I believe, as late as the end of the fourth century:—"Ne nunc quidem in eadem urbe Doctrinæ variæ silent, non apud nos exaruit Musica nec Harmonia conticuit." Lib. 22.

Page 25.—From the character of the features of the Sphinx, and a passage in Herodotus, describing the Egyptians as μελαγχροες και ουλοτρικες, Volney, Bruce, and a few others, have conclud- ed that the ancient inhabitants of Egypt were negroes. But this opinion is contradicted by a host of authorities. See *Castera*'s notes upon *Browne's Travels*, for the result of Blumenbach's [310] dissection of a variety of mummies. Denon, speaking of the character of the heads represented in the ancient sculpture and painting of Egypt, says, "Celle des femmes ressemble encore à la figure des jolies femmes d'aujourd'hui: de la rondeur, de la volupté, le nez petit, les yeux longs, peu ouverts," &c. &c. He could judge, too, he says, from the female mummies, "que leurs cheveux étoient longs et lisses, que le caractère de tête de la plupart tenoit du beau style"—"Je raportai," he adds, "une tête de vieille femme qui étoit aussi belle que celles de Michel Ange, et leur ressembloit beaucoup."

In a "*Description générale de Thèbes*" by *Messrs. Jollois et Desvilliers*, they say, "Toutes les sculptures Egyptiennes, depuis les plus grands colosses de Thèbes jusqu'aux plus petites idoles, ne rappellent en aucune manière les traits de la figure des nègres; outre que les têtes des momies des catacombs de Thèbes presentent des profils droits." See also *M. Jomard*'s "Description of Syene and the Cataracts," *Baron Larrey*, on the "conformation physique" of the Egyptians, &c.

De Pauw, the great depreciator of every thing Egyptian, has, on the authority of a passage in Ælian, presumed to affix to the countrywomen of Cleopatra the stigma of complete and unredeemed ugliness. The following line of Euripides, however, is an answer to such charges:—

Νειλου μεν αἱδε καλλιπαρθενοι ροαι.

In addition to the celebrated instances of Cleopatra, Rhodope, &c. we are told, on the authority of Manetho (as given by Zoega from Georgius Syncellus), of a beautiful queen of Memphis, Nitocris, of the sixth dynasty, who, in addition to other charms and perfections, was (rather inconsistently with the negro hypothesis) ξανθη την χροιαν.

[311]

See, for a tribute to the beauty of the Egyptian women, Montesquieu's Temple de Gnide.

Page 35.—"*Among beds of lotus flowers.*"—v. *Strabo.*

Page 36.—"*Isle of the golden Venus.*"—"On trouve une île appelée Venus-Dorée, ou le champ d'or, avant de remonter jusqu'à Memphis." *Voyages de Pythagore.*

Page 39.—For an account of the Table of Emerald, v. *Lettres sur l'Origine des Dieux d'Egypte. De Pauw* supposes it to be a modern fiction of the Arabs. Many writers have fancied that the art of making gold was the great secret that lay hid under the forms of Egyptian theology. "La science Hermétique," says the Benedictine, Pernetz, "l'art sacerdotal étoit la source de toutes les richesses des Rois d'Egypte, et l'objet de ces mystères si cachés sous le voile du leur pretendu Religion." *Fables Egyptiennes.* The hieroglyphs, that formerly covered the Pyramids, are supposed by some of these writers to relate to the same art. See *Mutus liber, Rupellæ.*

Page 40.—"By reflecting the sun's rays," says *Clarke,* speaking of the Pyramids, "they appeared white as snow."

Page 41.—For Bubastis, the Diana of the Egyptians, v. *Jablonski,* lib. 3. c. 4.

Page 43.—"*The light coracle,*" &c.—v. *Amuilhon,* "*Histoire de la Navigation et du Commerce des Egyptiens sous les Ptolemées.*" See also, for a description of the various kinds of boats used on the Nile, *Maillet,* tom. i. p. 98.

Page 44.—v. *Maurice,* Appendix to "Ruins of Babylon." [312] Another reason, he says, for their worship of the Ibis, "founded on their love of geometry, was (according to Plutarch) that the space between its legs, when parted asunder, as it walks, together with its beak, forms a complete equilateral triangle." From the examination of the embalmed birds, found in the Catacombs of Saccara, there seems to be no doubt that the Ibis was the same kind of bird as that described by Bruce, under the Arabian name of Abou Hannes.

Ib.—"*The sistrum,*" &c.—"Isis est genius," says *Servius,* "Ægypti, qui per sistri motum, quod gerit in dextra, Nili accessus recessusque significat."

Page 48.—"*The ivy encircled it*," &c.—The ivy was consecrated to Osiris. v. *Diodor. Sic.* 1. 10.

Ib.—"*The small mirror.*"—"Quelques unes," says *Dupuis*, describing the processions of Isis, "portoient des miroirs attachés à leurs épaules, afin de multiplier et de porter dans tous les sens les images de la Déesse." *Origine des Cultes*, tom. 8. p. 847. A mirror, it appears, was also one of the emblems in the mysteries of Bacchus.

Page 49.—"*There is, to the north of Memphis*," &c.—"Tout prouve que la territoire de Sakkarah étoit la Necropolis au sud de Memphis, et le faubourg opposé à celui-ci, où sont les pyramides de Gizeh, une autre Ville des Morts, qui terminoit Memphis au nord." *Denon.*

There is nothing known with certainty as to the site of Memphis, but it will be perceived that the description of its position given by the Epicurean corresponds, in almost every particular, with that which M. Maillet (the French consul, for many years, at Cairo) has left us. It must be always borne in mind, too, that of the distances between the respective places here mentioned, we have no longer any accurate means of judging.

[313]

Page 49.—"*Pyramid beyond pyramid.*"—"Multas olim pyramidas fuisse e ruinis arguitur." *Zoega.*—*Vansleb*, who visited more than ten of the small pyramids, is of opinion that there must have originally been a hundred in this place.

See, for the lake to the northward of Memphis, *Shaw's Travels*, p. 302.

Page 57.—"*The Theban beetle.*"—"On voit en Egypte, après la retraite du Nil et la fécondation des terres, le limon couvert d'une multitude de scarabées. Un pareil phénomène a dû sembler aux Egyptiens le plus propre à peindre une nouvelle existence." *M. Jomard.*—Partly for the same reason, and partly for another, still more fanciful, the early Christians used to apply this emblem to Christ. "Bonus ille scarabæus meus," says St. Augustine "non eâ tantum de causâ quod unigenitus, quod ipsemet sui auctor mortalium speciem induerit, sed quod in hac nostrâ fæce sese volutaverit et ex hac ipsa nasci voluerit."

Ib.—*"Enshrined within a case of crystal."*—"Les Egyptiens ont fait aussi, pour conserver leurs morts, des caisses de verre." *De Pauw.*—He mentions, in another place, a sort of transparent substance, which the Ethiopians used for the same purpose, and which was frequently mistaken by the Greeks for glass.

Page 58.—*"Among the emblems of death."*—"Un prêtre, qui brise la tige d'une fleur, des oiseaux qui s'envolent sont les emblemes de la morte et de l'âme qui se sépare du corps." *Denon.* [314]

Theseus employs the same image in the Phædra:—

Ορνις γαρ ὡς τις εκ χερων αφαντος ει
Πηδημ' ες ἁδου πικρον ὁρμησασα μοι.

Page 59.—"The singular appearance of a Cross so frequently recurring among the hieroglyphics of Egypt, had excited the curiosity of the Christians at a very early period of ecclesiastical history; and as some of the Priests, who were acquainted with the meaning of the hieroglyphics, became converted to Christianity the secret transpired. 'The converted heathens,' says Socrates Scholasticus, 'explained the symbol, and declared that it signified Life to Come.' " *Clarke.*

Lipsius, therefore, erroneously supposes the Cross to have been an emblem peculiar to the Christians. See, on this subject, *L'Histoire des Juifs*, liv. 9. c. 16.

It is singular enough that while the Cross was held sacred among the Egyptians, not only the custom of marking the forehead with the sign of the Cross, but Baptism and the consecration of the bread in the Eucharist were imitated in the mysterious ceremonies of Mithra. *Tertull. de Proscriptione Hereticorum.*

Zoega is of opinion that the Cross found (for the first time, it is said) on the destruction of the temple of Serapis, by the Christians, could have not been the crux ansata; as nothing is more common than this emblem on all the Egyptian monuments.

[315]

Page 62.—*"Stood shadowless."*—It was an idea entertained among the ancients that the Pyramids were so constructed ("mecanicâ constructione," says *Ammianus Marcellinus*) as never to cast any shadow.

Page 64.—*"Rhodope."*—From the story of Rhodope, Zoega thinks, "videntur Arabes ansam arripuisse ut in una ex pyramidibus, genii loco, habitare dicerent mulierem nudam insignis pulchritudinis quæ aspectu suo homines insanire faciat." *De Usu Obeliscorum.* See also *L'Egypte de Murtadi par Vattier.*

Page 66.—*"The Gates of Oblivion."*—"Apud Memphim æneas quasdam portas, quæ Lethes et Cocyti (hoc est oblivionis et lamentationis) appellenter aperiri, gravem asperumque edentes sonum." *Zoega.*

Page 69.—*"A pile of lifeless bodies."*—See, for the custom of burying the dead upright ("post funus stantia busto corpora," as Statius describes it), Dr. Clarke's preface to the 2d section of his fifth volume. They used to insert precious stones in the place of the eyes. "Les yeux étoient formés d'émeraudes, de turquoises," &c.—v. *Masoudy*, quoted by *Quatremere.*

Page 72.—*"It seemed as if every echo."*—See, for the echoes in the pyramids, *Plutarch, de Placitis Philosoph.*

Page 74.—*"Pale phantom-like shapes."*—"Ce moment heureux (de l'Autopsie) étoit preparé par des scènes effrayantes, par des alternatives de crainte et de joie, de lumière et des ténèbres, par la lueur des éclairs, par le bruit terrible de la foudre, qu'on imitoit, et par des apparitions de spectres, des illusions magiques, qui frappoient les yeux et les oreilles tout ensemble." *Dupuis.*

Page 77.—*"Serpents of fire."*—"Ces considérations me portent à penser que, dans les mystères, ces phénomènes étoient [316] beaucoup mieux exécutées et sans comparison plus terribles à l'aide de quelque composition pyrique, qui est restée cachée, comme celle du feu Grégeois." *De Pauw.*

Page 78.—*"The burning of the reed-beds of Ethiopia."*—"Il n'y a point d'autre moyen que de porter le feu dans ces forêts de roseaux, qui répandent alors dans tout le païs une lumière aussi considérable que celle du jour même." *Maillet*, tom. 1. p. 63.

Page 79.—*"The sound of torrents."*—The Nile, *Pliny* tells us, was admitted into the Pyramid.

Page 81.—*"I had almost given myself up."*—"On exerçoit," says *Dupuis*, "les recipiendaires, pendant plusieurs jours, à traverser, à la nage, une grande étendue d'eau. On les y jettoit et ce n'étoit que avec peine qu' ils s'en retiroient. On appliquoit le fer et le feu sur leurs membres. On les faisoit passer à travers les flammes."

The aspirants were often in considerable danger, and Pythagoras, we are told, nearly lost his life in the trials. v. *Recherches sur les Initiations, par Robin.*

Page 90.—For the two cups used in the mysteries, see *L'Histoire des Juifs*, liv. 9. c. 16.

Ib.—*"Osiris."*—Osiris, under the name of Serapis, was supposed to rule over the subterranean world; and performed the office of Pluto, in the mythology of the Egyptians. "They believed," says Dr. Pritchard, "that Serapis presided over the region of departed souls, during the period of their absence, when languishing without bodies, and that the dead were deposited in his palace." *Analysis of the Egyptian Mythology.*

[317]

Ib.—"*To cool the lips of the dead.*"—"Frigidam illam aquam post mortem, tanquam Hebes poculum, expetitam." *Zoega.*—The Lethe of the Egyptians was called Ameles. See *Dupuis*, tom. 8. p. 651.

Page 90.—"*A draught divine.*"—*Diodor. Sicul.*

Page 93.—"*Grasshopper, symbol of initiation.*"—*Hor. Apoll.*—The grasshopper was also consecrated to the sun as being musical.

Page 94.—"*Isle of gardens.*"—The isle Antirrhodus near Alexandria. *Maillet.*

Ib.—"*Vineyard at Anthylla.*"—See *Athen. Deipnos.*

Page 97.—"*We can see those stars.*"—"On voyoit en plein jour par ces ouvertures les étoiles, et même quelques planètes en leur plus grande latitude septentrionale; et les prêtres avoient bientôt profité de ce phénomène pour observer à diverses heures la passage des étoiles." *Séthos.*—*Strabo* mentions certain caves or pits, constructed for the purpose of astronomical observations, which lay in the Zelopolitan prefecture, beyond Heliopolis.

Page 98.—"*A plantain.*"—This tree was dedicated to the Genii of the Shades, from its being an emblem of repose and cooling airs. "Cui imminet musæ folium, quod ab Iside infera geniisque ei addictis manu geri solitum, umbram requiemque et auras frigidas subindigitare videtur." *Zoega.*

Page 107.—*"He spoke of the preexistence of the soul,"* &c.—For a full account of the doctrines which are here represented as having been taught to the initiated in the Egyptian [318] mysteries, the reader may consult *Dupuis, Pritchard's Analysis of the Egyptian Mythology*, &c. &c. "L'on découvroit l'origine de l'ame, sa chute sur la terre, à travers les sphères et les élémens, et son retour au lieu de sa origine ... c'étoit ici la partie la plus métaphysique, et que ne pourroit guère entendre le commun des Initiés, mais dont on lui donnoit le spectacle par des figures et des spectres allégoriques." *Dupuis.*

Page 108.—*"Those fields of radiance."*—See *Beausobre*, liv. 3. c. 4. for the "terre bienheureuse et lumineuse" which the Manicheans supposed God to inhabit. Plato, too, speaks (in Phæd.) of a "pure land lying in the pure sky (την γην καθαραν εν καθαρω κεισθαι ουρανω), the abode of divinity, of innocence, and of life."

Page 110.—*"Tracing it from the first moment of earthward desire."*—In the original construction of this work, there was an episode introduced here, (which I have since published in another form,) illustrating the doctrine of the fall of the soul by the Oriental fable of the Loves of the Angels.

Page 111.—*"Restoring her lost wings."*—*Damascius* in his Life of Isidorus, says, "Ex antiquissimis Philosophis Pythagoram et Platonem Isidorus ut Deos coluit, et *eorum animas alatas esse* dixit quas in locum supercœlestem inque campum veritatis et pratum elevatas, divinis putavit ideis pasci." *Apud Phot. Bibliothec.*

Page 112.—*"A pale, moonlike meteor."*—*Apuleius*, in describing the miraculous appearances exhibited in the mysteries, says, "Nocte mediâ vidi solem candido coruscantem lumine." *Metamorphos.* lib. 11. [319]

Page 113.—*"So entirely did the illusion of the scene,"* &c.—In tracing the early connection of spectacles with the ceremonies of religion, Voltaire says, "Il y a bien plus; les véritables grandes tragédies, les representations imposantes et terribles, étoient les mystères sacrés, qu'on célébroit dans les plus vastes temples du monde, en présence des seuls Initiés; c'étoit là que les habits, les décorations, les machines étoient propres au sujet; et le sujet étoit la vie présente et la vie future." *Des divers changemens arrivés à l'art tragique.*

To these scenic representations in the Egyptian mysteries, there is evidently an allusion in the vision of Ezekiel, where the spirit shows him the abominations which the Israelites learned in Egypt:—"Then said he unto me, 'Son of man, hast thou seen what the ancients of the house of Israel do in the dark, every man in *the chambers of his imagery.*'" Chap. 8.

Page 118.—*"The seven tables of stone."*—"Bernard, Comte de la Marche Trévisane, instruit par la lecture des livres anciens, dit qu' Hermes trouva sept tables dans la vallée d'Hebron, sur lesquelles étoient gravés les principes des arts liberaux." *Fables Egyptiennes.* See *Jablonski de stelis Herm.*

Page 119.—*"Beside the goat of Mendes."*—For an account of the animal worship of the Egyptians, see *De Pauw*, tom. 2.

Ib.—*"The Isiac serpents."*—"On auguroit bien des serpens Isiaques, lorsqu'ils goutoient l'offrande et se trainoient lentement autour de l'autel." *De Pauw.*

Page 121.—*"Hence the festivals and hymns,"* &c.—For an account of the various festivals at the different periods of the sun's progress, in the spring, and in the autumn, see *Dupuis* and *Pritchard.*

Ib.—*"The mysteries of the night."*—v. *Athenag. Leg. pro Christ.* p. 133.

Page 125.—*"A peal like that of thunder."*—See, for some curious remarks on the mode of imitating thunder and lightning in the ancient mysteries, *De Pauw*, tom. 1. p. 323. The machine with which these effects were produced on the stage was called a ceraunoscope.

Page 131.—*"Windings, capriciously intricate."*—In addition to the accounts which the ancients have left us of the prodigious excavations in all parts of Egypt,—the fifteen hundred chambers under the Labyrinth—the subterranean stables of the Thebaïd, containing a thousand horses—the crypts of Upper Egypt passing under the bed of the Nile, &c. &c.—the stories and traditions current among the Arabs still preserve the memory of those wonderful substructions. "Un Arabe," says Paul Lucas, "qui étoit avec nous, m'assura qu'étant entré autrefois dans le Labyrinthe, il avoit marché dans les chambres souterraines jusqu'en un lieu où il y avoit une grande place environnée de plusieurs niches qui ressembloit à de petites boutiques, d'où l'on entroit dans d'autres allées et dans des chambres, sans pouvoir en trouver la fin." In speaking, too, of the arcades along the Nile, near Cosseir, "Ils me dirent même que ces souterrains étoient si profondes qu'il y en avoient qui alloient à trois journées de là, et qu'ils conduisoient dans un pays où l'on voyoit de beaux jardins, qu'on y trouvoit de belles maisons," &c. &c.

See also in *M. Quatremere's Memoires sur l'Egypte*, tom. 1. p. 142., an account of a subterranean reservoir, said to have been discovered at Kaïs, and of the expedition undertaken by a party of persons, in a long narrow boat, for the purpose of exploring it. "Leur voyage avoit été de six jours, dont les quatre premiers furent employés à pénétrer les bords; les deux autres à revenir au lieu d'où ils étoient partis: Pendant tout cet intervalle ils ne [321] purent atteindre l'extrémité du bassin. L'émir Ala-eddin-Tam-boga, gouverneur de Behnesa, écrivit ces détails au sultan, qui en fut extrêmement surpris."

Page 136.—"*A small island in the centre of Lake Mœris.*"—The position here given to Lake Mœris, in making it the immediate boundary of the city of Memphis to the south, corresponds exactly with the site assigned to it by Maillet:—"Memphis avoit encore à son midi un vaste reservoir, par où tout ce qui peut servir à la commodité et à l'agrément de la vie lui étoit voituré abondamment de toutes les parties de l'Egypte. Ce lac qui la terminoit de ce côté-là," &c. &c. Tom. 2. p. 7.

Ib.—"*Ruins rising blackly above the wave.*"—"On voit sur la rive orientale des antiquités qui sont presque entièrement sous les eaux." *Belzoni.*

Page 137.—"*Its thundering portals.*"—"Quorundam autem domorum (in Labyrintho) talis est situs, ut adaperientibus foris tonitru intus terribile existat." *Pliny.*

Page 138.—"*Leaves that serve as cups.*"—*Strabo.* According to the French translator of Strabo, it was the fruit of the *faba Ægyptiaca*, not the leaf, that was used for this purpose. "Le κιβωριον," he says, "devoit s'entendre de la capsule ou fruit de cette plante, dont les Egyptiens se servoient comme d'un vase, imaginant que l'eau du Nil y devenoit delicieuse."

Page 142.—"*The fish of these waters,*" &c.—*Ælian,* lib. 6. 32.

Ib.—"*Pleasure boats or yachts.*"—Called Thalamages, from the pavilion on the deck. v. *Strabo.*

Page 144.—"*Covered with beds of those pale, sweet roses.*"—As April is the season for gathering these roses (See

Malte-brun's Economical Calendar), the Epicurean could not, of course, mean to say that he saw them actually in flower.

Page 146.—"*The lizards upon the bank.*"—"L'or et l'azur brillent en bandes longitudinales sur leur corps entier, et leur queue est du plus beau bleu celeste." *Sonnini.*

Page 147.—"*The canal through which we now sailed.*"—"Un canal," says *Maillet*, "très profond et très large y voituroit les eaux du Nil."

Page 150.—"*For a draught of whose flood,*" &c.—"Anciennement on portoit les eaux du Nil jusqu'au des contrées fort éloignées, et surtout chez les princesses du sang des Ptolomées, mariées dans des families étrangères." *De Pauw.*

Page 154.—"*Bearing each the name of its owner.*"—"Le nom du maître y étoit écrit, pendant la nuit en lettres de feu." *Maillet.* [323]

Page 155.—"*Cups of that frail crystal*"—called Alassontes. For their brittleness *Martial* is an authority:—

Tolle, puer, calices, tepidique toreumata Nili,
Et mihi securâ pocula trade manu.

Ib.—*"Bracelets of the black beans of Abyssinia."*—The bean of the Glycyne, which is so beautiful as to be strung into necklaces and bracelets, is generally known by the name of the black bean of Abyssinia. *Niebhur.*

Ib.—*"Sweet lotus-wood flute."*—See *M. Villoteau on the musical instruments of the Egyptians.*

Page 156.—*"Shine like the brow of Mount Atlas at night."*—*Solinus* speaks of the snowy summit of Mount Atlas glittering with flames at night. In the account of the Periplus of Hanno, as well as in that of Eudoxus, we read that as those navigators were coasting this part of Africa, torrents of light were seen to fall on the sea.

Page 158.—*"The tears of Isis."*—"Per lacrymas, vero, Isidis intelligo effluvia quædam Lunæ, quibus tantam vim videntur tribuisse Ægypti." *Jablonski.*—He is of opinion that the superstition of the *Nucta*, or miraculous drop, is of a relic of the veneration paid to the dews, as the tears of Isis.

Page 158.—*"The rustling of the acacias,"* &c.—*Travels of Captain Mangles.*

Ib.—*"Supposed to rest in the valley of the moon."*—*Plutarch. Dupuis*, tom. 10. The Manicheans held the same belief. See *Beausobre*, p. 565.

Page 160.—*"Sothis, the fair star of the waters."*—ὑδραγωγον is the epithet applied to this star by *Plutarch, de Isid.*

Ib.—*"Was its birth-star."*—Ἡ Σωθεως ανατολη γενεσεως καταρχουσα της εις τον κοσμον. *Porphyr. de Antro Nymph.*

Page 168.—*"Golden Mountains."*—v. *Wilford on Egypt and the Nile*, Asiatic Researches.

Ib.—*"Sweet-smelling wood."*—"'A l'époque de la crue le Nil Vert charie les planches d'un bois qui a une odeur semblable à celle de l'encens." *Quatremere.*

Page 169.—*"Barges full of bees."*—*Maillet.*

Page 170.—*"Such a profusion of the white flowers,"* &c.—"On les voit comme jadis cueillir dans les champs des tiges du lotus, signes du débordement et présages de l'abondance; ils s'enveloppent les bras et le corps avec les longues tiges fleuries, et parcourent les rues," &c. *Description des Tombeaux des Rois, par M. Costaz.*

Page 173.—*"While composing his commentary on the scriptures."*—It was during the composition of his great critical work, the Hexapla, that Origen employed these female scribes.

Page 176.—*"That rich tapestry,"* &c.

Non ego prætulerim Babylonica picta superbè
Texta, Semiramiâ quæ variantur acu.

Martial.   [325]

Page 200.—*"The Place of Weeping."*—v. *Wilford, Asiatic Researches*, vol. 3. p. 340.

Page 210.—*"We had long since left this mountain behind."*—The voyages on the Nile are, under favourable circumstances, performed with considerable rapidity. "En cinq ou six jours," says *Maillet*, "on pourroit aisément remonter de l'embouchure du Nil à ses cataractes, ou descendre des cataractes jusqu'à la mer." The great uncertainty of the navigation is proved by what *Belzoni* tells us:—"Nous ne mîmes cette fois que deux jours et demi pour faire le trajet du Caire à Melawi, auquel, dans notre second voyage, nous avions employés dix-huit jours."

Page 212.—"*Those mighty statues, that fling their shadows.*"—"Elles out près de vingt mètres (61 pieds) d'élévation; et au lever du soleil, leurs ombres immenses s'étendent au loin sur la chaine Libyen." *Description générale de Thèbes, par Messrs. Jollois et Desvilliers.*

Ib.—"*Those cool alcoves.*"—*Paul Lucas.*

Page 219.—"*Whose waters are half sweet, half bitter.*"—*Paul Lucas.*

Page 224.—"*The Mountain of the Birds.*"—There has been much controversy among the Arabian writers, with respect to the site of this mountain, for which see *Quatremere*, tom. 1. art. *Amoun.*

Page 230.—"*The hand of labour had succeeded,*" &c.—The monks of Mount Sinai (*Shaw* says) have covered over near four acres of the naked rocks with fruitful gardens and orchards.

Page 233.—"*The image of a head.*"—There was usually, Tertullian tells us, the image of Christ on the communion-cups.

Ib.—"*Kissed her forehead.*"—"We are rather disposed to infer," says the present Bishop of Lincoln, in his very sensible work on Tertullian, "that, at the conclusion of all their meetings for the purpose of devotion, the early Christians were accustomed to give the kiss of peace, in token of the brotherly love subsisting between them."

Page 237.—"*In the middle of the seven valleys.*"—See Macrizy's account of these valleys, given by Quatremere, tom. 1. p. 450.

Ib.—"*Red lakes of Nitria.*"—For a striking description of this region, see "*Rameses,*"—a work which, though, in general, too technical and elaborate, shows, in many passages, to what picturesque effects the scenery and mythology of Egypt may be made subservient.

Page 238.—"*In the neighbourhood of Antinoë.*"—From the position assigned to Antinoë in this work, we should conclude that it extended much farther to the north, than these few ruins of it that remain would seem to indicate; so as to render the distance between the city and the Mountain of the Birds considerably less than what it appears to be at present.

Page 243.—"*When Isis, the pure star of lovers.*"—v. *Plutarch de Isid.*

Ib.—"*Ere she again embrace her bridegroom sun.*"—"Conjunctio solis cum luna, quod est veluti utriusque connubium." *Jablonski.*   [327]

Page 247.—"*Of his walks a lion is the companion.*"—M. Chateaubriand has introduced Paul and his lion into the "*Martyrs,*" liv. 11.

Page 235.—"*Come thus secretly before day-break.*"—It was among the accusations of Celsus against the Christians, that they held their assemblies privately and contrary to law; and one of the speakers in the curious work of Minucius Felix calls the Christians "latebrosa et lucifugax natio."

Page 256.—"*A swallow,*" &c.—"Je vis dans le desert des hirondelles d'un gris clair comme le sable sur lequel elles volent."—*Denon.*

Page 257.—"*The comet that once desolated this world.*"—In alluding to Whiston's idea of a comet having caused the deluge, *M. Girard*, having remarked that the word Typhon means a deluge, adds, "On ne peut entendre par le tems du règne de Typhon que celui pendant lequel le déluge inonda la terre, tems pendant lequel on dût observer la comète qui l'occasionna, et dont l'apparition fut, non seulement pour les peuples de l'Egypte, et de l'Ethiopie, mais encore pour tous les peuples le présage funeste de leur destruction presque totale." *Description de la Vallée de l'E'garement.*

Page 259.—"*In which the spirit of my dream*," &c.—"Many people," said *Origen*, "have been brought over to Christianity by the Spirit of God giving a sudden turn to their minds, and offering visions to them either by day or night." On this *Jortin* remarks:—"Why should it be thought improbable that Pagans of good dispositions, but not free from prejudices, should have been called by divine admonitions, by dreams or visions, which might be a support to Christianity in those days of distress."

[328]

Page 263.—"*One of those earthen cups.*"—*Palladius*, who lived some time in Egypt, describes the monk Ptolemæus, who inhabited the desert of Scete, as collecting in earthen cups the abundant dew from the rocks.—*Bibliothec. Pat.* tom. 13.

Page 264.—"*It was to preserve, he said*," &c.—The brief sketch here given of the Jewish dispensation agrees very much with the view taken of it by Dr. Sumner, the present Bishop of Llandaff, in the first chapters of his eloquent and luminous work, the "Records of the Creation."

Page 266.—"*In vain did I seek the promise of immortality.*"—"It is impossible to deny," says the Bishop of Llandaff, "that the sanctions of the Mosaic Law are altogether temporal.... It is, indeed, one of the facts that can only be explained by acknowledging that he really acted under a divine commission, promulgating a temporary law for a peculiar purpose,"—a much more candid and sensible way of treating this very difficult point, than by either endeavouring, like Warburton, to escape from it into a paradox, or still worse, contriving, like Dr. Graves, to increase its difficulty by explanation. v. *"On the Pentateuch."* See also *Horne's Introduction, &c.* vol. I. p. 226.

Page 268.—*"All are of the dust,"* &c.—While Voltaire, Volney, &c. refer to the Ecclesiastes, as abounding with tenets of materialism and Epicurism, Mr. Des Voeux and others find in it strong proofs of belief in a future state. The chief difficulty lies in the chapter from which this text is quoted; and [329] the mode of construction by which some writers attempt to get rid of it,—namely, by putting these texts into the mouth of a foolish reasoner,—appears forced and gratuitous. v. *Dr. Hales's Analysis.*

Page 270.—*"The noblest and first-created,"* &c.—This opinion of the Hermit may be supposed to have been derived from his master, Origen; but it is not easy to ascertain the exact doctrine of Origen on this subject. In the Treatise on Prayer attributed to him, he asserts that God the Father alone should be invoked,—which, says Bayle, is "encherir sur les Hérésies des Sociniens." Notwithstanding this, however, and some other indications of, what was afterwards called, Arianism, (such as the opinion of the divinity being received by *communication,* which *Milner* asserts to have been held by this Father,) Origen was one of the authorities quoted by Athanasius in support of his high doctrines of co-eternity and co-essentiality. What Priestley says is, perhaps, the best solution of these inconsistencies;—"Origen, as well as Clemens Alexandrinus, has been thought to favour the Arian principle; but he did it only in words and not in ideas." *Early Opinions, &c.* Whatever uncertainty, however, there may exist with respect to the opinion of Origen himself on this subject, there is no doubt that the doctrines of his immediate followers were, at least, Anti-Athanasian. "So many Bishops of Africa," says Priestley, "were, at this period (between the years 255 and 258), Unitarians, that Athanasius says, 'The Son of God,'—meaning his divinity,—'was scarcely any longer preached in the churches.' "

Page 271.—*"The restoration of the whole human race to purity and happiness."*—This benevolent doctrine,—which not only goes far to solve the great problem of moral and physical evil, but which would, if received more generally, tend to soften the spirit of uncharitableness, so fatally prevalent among Christian sects,—was maintained by that great light of the early Church, Origen, and has not wanted supporters among more modern Theologians. That Tillotson was inclined to the opinion appears from his sermon preached before the queen. Paley is supposed to have held the same amiable doctrine; and Newton (the author of the work on the Prophecies) is also among the supporters of it. For a full account of the arguments in favour of this opinion, derived both from reason and the express language of Scripture, see Dr. Southwood Smith's very interesting work, "On the Divine Government." See also *Magee on the Atonement*, where the doctrine of the advocates of Universal Restoration is thus briefly and fairly explained:—"Beginning with the existence of an infinitely powerful, wise, and good Being, as the first and fundamental principle of rational religion, they pronounce the essence of this Being to be *love*, and from this infer, as a demonstrable consequence, that none of the creatures formed by such a Being will ever be made eternally miserable.... Since God (they say) would act unjustly in inflicting eternal misery for temporary crimes, the sufferings of the wicked can be but remedial, and will terminate in a complete purification from moral disorder, and in their ultimate restoration to virtue and happiness."

Page 273.—*"Fruit of the desert shrub."*—v. Hamilton's *Ægyptiaca*.

Page 278.—"*The white garment she wore, and the ring of gold on her finger.*"—See, for the custom among the early Christians of wearing white for a few days after baptism, *Ambros. de Myst.*—With respect to the ring, the Bishop of Lincoln says, in his work on Tertullian, "The natural inference from these words (*Tertull. de Pudicitiâ*) appears to be that a ring used to be given in baptism; but I have found no other trace of such a custom." [331]

Page 280.—"*Pebbles of jasper.*"—v. *Clarke.*

Ib.—"*Stunted marigold,*" &c.—"Les *Mesembryanthemum nodiflorum* et *Zygophyllum coccineum,* plantes grasses des déserts, rejetées à cause de leur âcreté par les chameaux, les chèvres, et les gazelles." *M. Delile upon the plants of Egypt.*

Page 281.—"*Antinoë.*"—v. *Savary* and *Quatremere.*

Page 286.—"*I have observed in my walks.*"—"Je remarquai avec une réflexion triste, qu'un animal de proie accompagne presque toujours les pas de ce joli et frêle individu."

Page 272.—"*Glistened over its silver letters.*"—The Codex Cottonianus of the New Testament is written in silver letters on a purple ground. The Codex Cottonianus of the Septuagint version of the Old Testament is supposed to be the identical copy that belonged to Origen.

Page 289.—"*Some denier of Christ.*"—Those Christians who sacrificed to idols to save themselves were called by various names, *Thurificati, Sacrificati, Mittentes, Negatores,* &c. Baronius mentions a bishop of this period (253), Marcellinus, who, yielding to the threats of the Gentiles, threw incense upon the altar. v. *Arnob. contra Gent.* lib. 7. [332]

Page 297.—"*The clear voice with which,*" &c.—The merit of the confession "Christianus sum," or "Christiana sum," was considerably enhanced by the clearness and distinctness with which it was pronounced. *Eusebius* mentions the martyr Vetius as making it λαμπροτατη φωνη.

Page 304.—*"The band round the young Christian's brow."*—We find poisonous crowns mentioned by *Pliny*, under the designation of "coronæ ferales." *Paschalius*, too, gives the following account of these "deadly garlands," as he calls them:—"Sed mirum est tam salutare inventum humanam nequitiam reperisse, quomodo ad nefarios usus traducent. Nempe, repertæ sunt nefandæ coronæ harum, quas dixi, tam salubrium per nomen quidem et speciem imitatrices, at re et effectu ferales, atque adeo capitis, cui imponuntur, interfectrices." *De Coronis.*

THE END.

LONDON:
Printed by A. & R. Spottiswoode,
New-Street-Square.

Transcriber's Note

Variations in hyphenation (e.g. "daybreak", "day-break", "over-head", "over-head") have not been changed.

In the notes, some references are to the wrong pages or out of sequence.

Other changes, which have been made to the text:

page 32, "alrea d" changed to "already"
page 81, "stirke" changed to "strike"
page 93, "grashopper" changed to "grasshopper"
page 188, quote mark added before "The state of misery"
page 194, "decome" changed to "become"
page 312, quote mark added before "There is, to the north of Memphis"

9 791041 940332